IF CATS DISAPPEARED
FROM THE WORLD

IF
CATS
DISAPPEARED
FROM
THE
WORLD

GENKI KAWAMURA

Translated from the Japanese by
Eric Selland

PICADOR

First published in the UK in paperback 2018 by Picador
an imprint of Pan Macmillan
20 New Wharf Road, London N1 9RR
Associated companies throughout the world
www.panmacmillan.com

ISBN 978-1-5098-8917-4

1 3 5 7 9 8 6 4 2

A CIP catalogue record for this book is available from the British Library.

Printed and bound by CPI Group (UK) Ltd, Croydon, CR0 4YY

Visit **www.picador.com** to read more about all our books
and to buy them. You will also find features, author interviews and
news of any author events, and you can sign up for e-newsletters
so that you're always first to hear about our new releases.

IF CATS DISAPPEARED
FROM THE WORLD

A SHORT INTRODUCTION

If cats disappeared from the world, how would the world change? And how would my life change?

And if I disappeared from the world? Well, I suppose nothing would change at all. Things would probably just go on, day after day . . . same as usual.

OK, so you're probably thinking this is all a bit silly, but please, believe me.

What I'm about to tell you happened over the past seven days.

Now that's what you call a weird week.

Oh, and by the way—I'm going to die soon.

So how did all this happen?

My letter will explain everything.

So it will probably be a long letter.

But I'd like you to bear with me till the end.

Because this will be my first and my last letter to you.

It's also my will and testament.

MONDAY: THE DEVIL MAKES
HIS APPEARANCE

I didn't even have ten things I wanted to do before I die.

In a movie I saw once the heroine is about to die so makes a list of ten things she wants to do before she goes.

What a lot of crap.

OK. So maybe I shouldn't be so harsh. But really, what even goes on a list like that? A load of rubbish probably.

"But how can you say that?" you might ask.

OK, look, I don't know, but anyway I tried it and it was just embarrassing.

It all started seven days ago.

I had this cold I just couldn't shake, but I kept going to work every day anyway, delivering the mail. I had a slight fever which wouldn't shift, and the right side of my head ached. I was barely keeping it together with the help of some over-the-counter drugs (I hate going to the doctor). But after two weeks of this I caved and went—I just wasn't getting better.

Then I found out it wasn't a cold.

It was, in fact, a brain tumor. Grade 4.

Anyway, that's what the doctor told me. He also told me I had only six months to live, tops. I'd be lucky if I made it another week. Then he explained my options—chemotherapy, anticancer drugs, palliative care . . . but I wasn't listening.

When I was little, I used to go to swimming. I'd jump into the cold blue water with a splash, and then sink, slowly.

"Do a proper warm-up before you jump in!" It was my mother's voice. But underwater it was muffled and hard to hear. For some reason this just popped into my head—this strange, noisy memory. Something I'd completely forgotten about until now.

Finally the appointment ended.

The doctor's words were still hanging in the air as I

dropped my bag on the floor and staggered out of the examining room. I ignored the doctor's shouts, calling for me to stop, and ran out of the hospital screaming. I ran and ran, slamming into the people I passed, falling over, rolling on the ground and getting up again, throwing my limbs about wildly until I reached the foot of a bridge where I found I could no longer move, and groveling on my hands and knees, let out a sob.

. . . Well, no, that's a lie. That's not quite how it happened.

The fact is, people tend to be surprisingly calm when they hear news like this.

When I found out, the first thing that occurred to me was that I was only one stamp away from getting a free massage on my loyalty card, and I shouldn't have bothered buying so much toilet paper and detergent. It was the little things which came to mind.

But finally, it hit me: a kind of bottomless sadness. I was only thirty. OK, so that would mean I'd have lived longer than Hendrix or Basquiat, but somehow it felt like I had a lot of unfinished business. There must be something, I don't know what, but something on this planet that only I could do.

But I didn't really dwell on any of this. Instead I wandered in a daze until I reached the station. A couple of young men were playing acoustic guitar and singing.

"This life will someday have to end, so until that final day arrives,
    Do what you want to do, do it, do all you can,
    That's how you face tomorrow."

Idiots. Now that's what you call a complete lack of imagination. Go ahead—just go on and sing your lives away in front of this godawful station.

I was so mad I couldn't take it. It was too much and I had no idea what to do. I took my time getting back to the flat. I clattered up the stairs and opened the flimsy door to the cramped little space which I called home. It was then that the complete hopelessness of it all caught up with me. The outlook was bad. I mean literally, I couldn't see a thing—I collapsed right there on the doorstep.

When I woke up I was still lying by the door. God knows how long I'd been there for. I could make out a black and white ball with grey patches in front of me. Then the ball made a sound—"miaow". Finally I realized it was the cat.

It has been me and him for four years now. He came closer and let out another "miaow". I took this as a sign he was worried about me. But hey, I wasn't dead yet, so I sat up. I still had a fever and my head was killing me: I really was sick.

Then suddenly someone's chirping from across the room.

"So great to meet you!"

And there I was. I mean, it was me, standing there, looking at me. Or someone who looked just like me. The word "doppelgänger" sprang to mind . . . I read something about this sort of thing in a book ages ago. It's another you who appears when you're about to die. Had I finally gone crazy, or was my time already up? My head was starting to spin, but I managed to keep it together. I decided to tackle head on whatever it was standing before me.

"Er, so, who are you?"

"Who do you think?"

"Uhh, is it . . . the Angel of Death?"

"Close!"

"Close?"

"I'm the Devil."

"The Devil?"

"Yes, the Devil!"

So that's how, in a slightly surprising way, the Devil appeared in my life.

Have you ever seen the Devil? Well, I have, and the real Devil doesn't have a scary red face or a pointy tail. And there's definitely no pitchfork! The Devil looks just like you. So the real doppelgänger was the Devil!

It was a lot to take in, but what choice did I have? Plus he seemed like a nice guy. So I decided that I'd just have to go along with it.

Upon closer inspection I realized that although the Devil looked a lot like me, we couldn't be more different when it came to our sense of style. I tend to dress in basic black and white. For instance, I'll wear black slacks with a white shirt and black jumper. Boring yes, but that's just who I am—the monotone guy. I remember ages ago my mother getting fed up—"There you go again buying the same kind of clothes as always . . .", but I'd still find myself choosing the same thing whenever I went shopping.

The Devil, though, dressed, um, shall we say, uncon-ventionally? Brightly colored Hawaiian shirts with palm trees or pictures of classic American cars, and he was always in shorts—like someone permanently on holiday. And of course, you mustn't forget the sunglasses (prob-ably Ray-Bans). He was dressed as if it were still summer despite the fact it was freezing out. Just as I was about to reach boiling point, the Devil spoke.

"So what are you going to do now?"

"Huh?"

"I mean, you haven't got a lot of time left . . . you know, this life-expectancy thing and all that."

"Oh that, right . . ."

"So what are you going to do?"

"Oh, well, for the time being maybe I'll think about that list of ten things . . ."

"You don't mean like that old movie, do you?"

"Mmm, yeah sort of, I guess . . ."

"You mean you'd really do something as silly and corny as that?"

"So you think it's a bad move?"

"Well, I mean, sure a lot of people do it, firmly declaring they'll do every last one . . . you know those kind of people, right? It's a kind of phase everyone goes through at least once—though it's not as if you get a second chance!"

Holding on to his sides, the Devil let out a huge guffaw.

"Sorry, I just can't see the funny side . . ."

"Right, right . . . Well, I guess you never know until you try, right? Let's draw up a quick list right now."

So I pulled out a sheet of blank paper and wrote the title at the top of the page—"10 Things I Want to Do Before I Die."

I was feeling more depressed already—I'm going to die soon and I'm wasting my time writing lists? You've got to be kidding. As I wrote I lost the plot even more. But somehow I managed to come up with a list, all the time avoiding the Devil, who was trying to peek over my shoulder, and forcibly removing the cat, who like all cats thinks it's a good idea to sit on whatever you're trying to work on or read.

OK, so here we go:
Go skydiving.
Climb Mt. Everest.
Speed along on the autobahn in a Ferrari.

Go along to a traditional three-day-long feast of
    gourmet Chinese food.
Take a ride on a Transformer's back.
Find love in these final Days of Our Lives.
Go on a date with Princess Leia.
Turn a corner just in time to run into a beautiful
    woman carrying a cup of coffee, and watch our
    passionate love affair unfold from there.
Run into the girl I had a crush on in school while
    sheltering from the rain.
Did I mention I'd like to fall in love? Just once . . .

"What *is* this?"

"Uh, well, you know . . ."

"C'mon, you're not in school anymore! Frankly, I'm embarrassed for you."

". . . Sorry."

Yeah I know, I'm pathetic. I racked my brains and this was the best I could come up with. Even the cat looked disgusted. He was keeping his distance.

The Devil came over and patted me on the shoulder, trying to cheer me up.

"There, there, now . . . OK, tell ya what, let's see

about that skydiving trip. A quick visit to the ATM and it's off to the airport we go!"

Two hours later I was on a jet plane at an altitude of 3,000 meters.

"OK, ready? Geronimo!"

Cheerful as ever, the Devil gave me a shove and the next thing I knew I was falling.

Yep. That's what I'd always dreamed of: to see the blue sky opening up, the towering clouds, and the earth's horizon stretching on forever . . . I'd always thought things would never be the same again after seeing the earth from so high up. I'd forget all the small stuff and grab life by the horns.

I'm sure some famous person said something like that, but that's not how it went. I'd had enough of the whole thing before I even jumped. I mean, come on, it's cold, you're way up there, and it's terrifying. Why would someone go and jump out of a plane of their own free will? Was *this* what I had wanted? I pondered these things as I fell to earth, before once again, things literally went literally black.

*

When I came to I was lying on my bed back home in my tiny apartment. Again it was the cat's "miaow" that woke me. Dragging myself up, I discovered my head was still killing me . . . I knew it. It was back down to earth with a bump.

"Oh, come on, man, give me a break . . . !" I pleaded with Aloha (as I'd decided the Devil, with his Hawaiian shirts, would henceforth be known), who sat next to me on the bed.

"My apologies for the inconvenience."

"Hey, I could've died out there . . . Well, OK, I realize I'm going to die anyway, but really . . ."

Aloha was splitting his sides.

I just kept quiet and held the cat in my arms. He felt warm and soft—a smooth, fluffy ball in my arms. Before, I would hold him and pet him without thinking about it much, but now, for the first time, it occurred to me that this is what life was all about.

"The thing is . . . I mean, there's just not many things I want to do before I die."

"Oh, really?"

"At least, I don't think I could think of ten. And the ones I can think of are probably really boring."

"Well, I guess that's life, huh?"

"Oh, by the way, could I ask you something?"

"Who, me?"

"Yeah, I was wondering . . . Why did you come? I mean . . . what are you doing here?"

Aloha let out a laugh. It could only mean bad things.

"You *really* want to know? Well, OK then, I'll tell you."

"OK, now you're scaring me."

I winced at the sudden change in Aloha's tone. I had a bad feeling about this. I could tell there was trouble up ahead.

"What's wrong?" Aloha asked.

I took a deep breath and steeled myself. It's OK. I'll be OK. I'm just asking a question. Nothing wrong with asking a question.

"Oh, nothing. It's fine. I'd just like to know. So go ahead. Shoot."

"So it turns out . . . you're going to die tomorrow."

"What!?"

"You're going to die tomorrow. That's what I came here to tell you."

14

I was speechless. Shock was followed swiftly by a feeling of deep despair. My whole body felt weak, and my knees trembled.

Seeing me in this state Aloha resumed his usual cheerful chit-chat.

"Hey, don't be so down. Look at me, I'm here to help! This is your way out. I've come to make you an offer."

". . . Way out? What do you mean?"

"You don't want to die *now*, do you? In your sorry state?"

"No, I want to live . . . if I can."

Without missing a beat Aloha went on:

"There is something we could do . . ."

"Do? What do you mean?"

"Well, you could call it a kind of magic. But it might increase your life span."

"Really?"

"On one condition: you'll have to accept this one fundamental law of the universe."

"And that is?"

"In order to gain something you have to lose something."

"So what do I have to do exactly?"

"It's easy . . . I'll just ask you to perform a simple exchange."

"Exchange?"

"Sure . . . All you have to do is remove one thing from the world, and in return, you get one more day of life."

"You're kidding. That's all?"

I may have been about to die, but I hadn't completely lost it yet. First of all, what gave Aloha the right to make such an offer?

"Now, you're probably wondering what gives me the right to do that."

"Um, uh . . . no, what made you say that?"

Was he for real? Did he have ESP?

"Reading minds is the easy part. Hello, I'm the Devil, remember?"

"Hmmmm."

"Anyway, we don't have much time, so you're going to have to get on board quickly. Are you with me? This is a real exchange we're talking about here."

"So says you."

"OK then. Since you don't believe me, let me tell you how this exchange came about."

Aloha made himself comfortable.

"You're familiar with the Book of Genesis?"

"You mean the Bible? Yes, I'm familiar with it, but I've never read it."

"Oh, wow, OK . . . this would have gone a lot faster if you had."

"Sorry . . ."

"Whatever . . . I'll just give it to you in condensed form. First of all, God created the world in seven days."

"Yeah, I've heard that bit."

"On the first day the world was covered in darkness, then God said, 'Let there be light!' and then there was day and night. Then, on the second day, God created the heavens, and on the third day he created the earth. Now that's what you call Creation! Then the oceans were made and plants took root."

"Pretty impressive."

"Right! And then, on the fourth day he created the sun and the moon and the stars in the sky—The. Universe. Is. Born! Then on the fifth day he created fish and birds, and on the sixth day he created animals, and made man in his own image, and finally that's your cue!"

"Oh, I remember now—creation of the heavens and the earth, the cosmos, and then humankind arrives on stage. And on the seventh day? What happens?"

"On the seventh day he rested. Even God needs to take a break now and then."

"And that's Sunday, right?"

"Exactly. Now isn't that incredible? He did it all in just seven days. God is just awesome! You know, I have so much respect for him."

Somehow when it came to what all this should inspire, respect didn't seem to cut it . . . but in any case, I decided to give him the benefit of the doubt.

"The first man's name was Adam. Then God thought he might be lonely since he was the only human around, so he created a woman from Adam's rib. But then the two of them were just hanging out there without much to do so I decided—to liven things up for them—to suggest to God that I get them to eat the apple."

"The apple?"

"Right. See, the two of them were living in the Garden of Eden, which was a kind of paradise where they could do anything they wanted, eat anything they wanted. But that's not all, there was no such thing as aging or death. There was just one thing they *weren't* allowed to do—to eat from the tree of the knowledge of good and evil. That's where the apple comes in . . . the forbidden fruit."

"I see."

"And so I suggested that they eat the apple, and they did!"

"No! Wow, you really are evil."

"Now, now, hold your applause. So the two of them were driven out of paradise. That meant that humans would be fated to experience aging and death, and so began a long history of conflict and struggle."

"Man, you really are the Devil."

"I appreciate your admiration, but it wasn't that much of a big deal. So somewhere along the way God sent his own son, Jesus Christ, down to earth, but not even that could convince human beings to take a cold hard look at themselves. Then to top it off, they go and kill this Jesus dude."

"Oh, yeah, I've heard about that part."

"Then after that, human beings just became more and more selfish. They started to make all sorts of new-fangled things—you know, all those little doodads you're not sure you really need, making more and more, going on and on . . ."

"I'm beginning to see."

"So I made another suggestion, you know, to God. So I say to him, look, how about I go down to earth and help those humans decide what it is they really need and what they don't need. And then, I made a promise to God. I said, whenever those humans decide to get rid of something, as a reward, I'll extend their life for one day. I was given the power to do that. So after that, I did a lot of searching. You know, for people I could do business with. And so that's where you find me—I've made deals with all kinds of people. As a matter of fact, you're number 108."

"Number 108?"

"That's right! Not that many, eh? Only 108 people in the whole world. You're pretty lucky, really. Simply by making one thing disappear from the world, you can extend your life by one day. Isn't that great?!"

It had come out of nowhere, and was such a ridiculous offer. He sounded just like the shopping channel on cable TV, desperate to sell you something. How can you extend your life by making such a simple swap? But on the other hand, setting aside for a moment the question of whether I actually believed it or not, I wasn't exactly in a position to refuse. Either way, I was going to die. I had no choice.

So, to recap: by making something disappear from the world, I could live for one more day. Let's see now, that would be thirty items a month, 365 per year.

It would be that simple. The world is basically drowning in crap—all those small, silly, useless things like the parsley they put on an omelet, or the promotional packs of tissues they give out in front of the train station. Or how about those lengthy users' manuals that come with your new fridge or washing machine. Or watermelon seeds. When you think about it, all kinds of unnecessary things spring to mind. When you weigh it up, there must be at least one or two million things the world could do without.

If I was supposed to live to seventy, that would mean I have forty more years left on the clock. So if I get rid of 14,600 items, I could make it to seventy after all. And if I kept going, I might even be able to reach a hundred, or even two hundred years old!

Just like Aloha said, for thousands of years, humankind has done nothing but make useless things. So if something were to disappear no one would notice. In fact, the world would be a simpler place. People will thank me for this!

And besides, just take a look at what I do for a living: a postman, a letter carrier. Pretty soon, postmen will be extinct. Because the day will come when letters and postcards disappear—they've been made redundant. When you think about it, there must be all kinds of things cluttering up the world which are borderline unnecessary. Maybe the entire human race is unnecessary. The world we live in has no meaning at all.

"OK. Fine. I agree to the exchange. Go ahead and make something disappear. I want to live longer." I accepted the terms. And once I'd made the decision to give up some of the things in my life, I suddenly felt a lot bolder.

"Oh, wow, really? Great! Now you're talking!"

Aloha seemed bowled over by my decision.

"Well, you're the one who came up with . . . Oh, whatever. So what should I erase? Hmmm, let's see . . . first of all, how about we get rid of these stains on the wall."

Aloha just stared blankly at me and said nothing.

"OK, how about the dust on top of the bookshelves?"

Again, silence.

"I know, let's get rid of that mold growing on the bathroom tiles!"

"C'mon now, what do you think I am, the maid? Let's not forget that it's the Devil you're working with."

"Oh, am I not thinking along the right lines?"

"What did you expect? I'm the one who gets to decide."

"And how do you do that?"

"How? Well, now that you ask, I suppose it's just a feeling, or depends on what mood I'm in."

"Mood?"

"Uh huh. So, what's it gonna be . . ."

Aloha surveyed the room. I followed his gaze, the whole time silently pleading: don't touch that figurine, and not those limited-edition trainers . . .

But obviously, when you think about it, I was being given my life in return for anything he might take. This is exactly what they mean when they talk about making a pact with the Devil—it's not supposed to be easy. So do I have to choose something really big to make disappear? The sun? Or the moon? The ocean, or the earth itself? Would that be enough for him? Just as I was finally realizing what a big deal this really was, Aloha's stare settled on the tabletop.

"What's this?"

Aloha grabbed the small packet and shook it. A rattling sound escaped from the box.

"Those are chocolate biscuits. You know, 'Mountain Mushrooms.'"

"Mushrooms?"

"No, 'Mountain Mushrooms.'"

This didn't seem to make any sense to Aloha, who tilted his head and looked puzzled.

"OK, then what's this?"

Aloha picked up a similar-looking box which was sitting next to the first one and gave it a shake. It made the same rattling sound.

"They're 'Bamboo Shoot Village' biscuits."

"Bamboo shoots?"

"No, not bamboo shoots, 'Bamboo Shoot Village.'"

"That makes no sense."

"Sorry. They're chocolate treats."

"Chocolate?"

"That's right."

I had won the boxes of chocolate in a raffle in the local shopping center a few days earlier (more like compensation for not winning the big prize), and they had sat there on the table ever since. When you think about it, it is kind of a weird concept for a brand of chocolate biscuits. It was no wonder the Devil was confused.

"Ah, yes. I've heard about how much humans love chocolate, but I didn't realize they'd taken it this far. Why in the shape of mushrooms and bamboo shoots?"

"Good question. I never thought about it before."

"OK . . . Well then. Shall we do the chocolates?"

"Huh?"

"We're deciding what's going to disappear from the world! Don't you remember?"

24

"Isn't that kind of a random choice?"

"Well, it is your first go at this . . ."

If chocolates disappeared from the world . . .

How would the world change? I tried to imagine what it might be like.

Let's see, chocolate addicts around the world would grieve, cry, and scream, and be overcome with loss. Then their blood-sugar levels would fall, and they would live out the rest of their lives in a state of lethargy.

In a world without chocolate, would marshmallows and caramel just take its place? Probably not, I don't think they have the same appeal as chocolate. And besides, people would get right to work on coming up with a new kind of sweet thing to replace chocolate with.

It just goes to show how insatiable we are when it comes to food.

The cat sat next to me eating the leftovers with rice that I'd just fed him. In Japanese, there's a whole other word for the food pets eat. It's just not the same as human food—we humans are way fussier.

Human beings put a lot of time and effort into what we eat, finding the right flavors, cooking, even making food into beautiful shapes. And chocolate is part of that too. Some chocolate has nuts in it, or comes in the form of a kind of biscuit or wafer. And in this case we've made it look like mushrooms and bamboo shoots. Chocolate seems to have really inspired us humans to come up with new ideas. Maybe that's what's driven all human progress: an insatiable desire for new things.

Something about all this made me feel like I've been lucky to have lived after all.

Now, you would have to be crazy to stand up and declare, "I would gladly give my life for chocolate!" I don't think there's anybody in the entire world who's that stupid. But if giving up chocolate can save my life, then why not? This is a stroke of luck. If that's all it takes then let's do it! There must be loads of similar things that I can easily give up to buy me more time.

Just as I was beginning to feel like my dealings with the Devil might really be offering me a speck of hope, Aloha spoke.

"So does this stuff taste good?" he said, gazing at the two boxes of chocolate biscuits.

"Not bad," I answered.

"Right . . ."

"Have you ever tried it?"

"No."

"Here, have one."

"No thanks. Human food just doesn't agree with me. It just all tastes . . . I don't know . . ."

"Oh really? Wow."

I was about to ask him more about what devils eat, but I decided to keep my curiosity in check. Then Aloha's curiosity seemed to get the best of him and he grabbed the box of "Mountain Mushrooms," took a whiff, and stared at the tiny biscuits. He smelled them again. Then he warily brought the biscuits to his lips, and scrunching his eyes shut, shoved one of them into his mouth.

Silence. A muffled, crunching sound. The room echoed with the sound of Aloha munching on chocolate biscuits.

"How is it?" I asked gently, but Aloha kept his eyes closed and stayed silent.

"So . . . how is it? Not good?"

Aloha seemed speechless, he let out a muffled munching sound.

"Are you OK?"

Again the muffled sound.

"Should I call an ambulance or something?"

"Mmmmff . . . wow that was so good!"

"Really?"

"What do they put in these things? They're just too

good! Are you sure you want to get rid of them? What a waste!"

"Wait a minute, I thought you said I should make them disappear."

"Well, I don't know about that. If I did, it must have been a mistake. I hadn't realized how delicious these things would be."

"But if I don't do something I'll die! Isn't that what you said?"

"Mmmm, well, you could put it like that."

"OK, then I'll get rid of them."

". . . Really?"

Aloha seemed genuinely sad, as he spoke his shoulders sagged.

"Yes, really."

I was beginning to feel sorry for him, but my answer was final.

"OK. But just one more!" Aloha burst out.

"What?"

"Can I have one more? This'll be the last one, I swear."

Aloha looked so pathetic, pleading as he was. His eyes began to well up with tears. It looked like he'd really taken a shine to chocolate. Stealthily, while he thought I wasn't looking, he grabbed a few more of the chocolates and stuffed them into his mouth, savoring the taste. When he was done he spoke again.

"Mmmm, yeah, ya know, I just can't do it."

"What?"

"It would be a crime to get rid of such a delicious thing."

"What the . . ."

How could he change his mind so easily? I mean, it's my life we're talking about here!

I thought I'd come to terms with the fact that I was going to die soon, but now that I'd been offered a way out, I found myself willing to try anything, no matter how ridiculous it seemed. When I do finally die, I'd like to go quietly, peacefully, and with dignity—that's how I always thought it would happen. But when you're suddenly faced with death, you find yourself willing to accept a helping hand from anyone, even the Devil, in order to stay alive. It's a basic human instinct. Dignity and respectability have gone out the window at that point.

"I'm not entirely OK with that."

"What's this now? Not having a crisis of conscience, are we?"

"What do you mean, of course I'm having a crisis! It's my life, and you think you can decide whether I live or die based on what you happen to fancy?"

"Why not? I mean, I *am* the Devil."

This was too much. I was speechless.

Aloha went on—

"Oh, come on! Don't look so depressed. I'll think of something else. I'll come up with something right away, tout de suite!"

With that, Aloha began to quickly scan the room. You could tell he was trying to make up for having chosen the wrong thing first time around.

Not that impressive for a devil, I thought. I gave him an icy stare as he continued his work. Then suddenly my mobile phone rang. Someone was calling from the post office where I work. I looked at the clock. It was well past the time I usually begin my shift.

The voice on the other end of the line belonged to my boss, the postmaster. He sounded annoyed and pointed out that I was late. The day before I'd left early to go to the clinic because I didn't feel well—actually he sounded kind of worried about me.

"I'm OK, but I could use some more time off to recover. Could I have the rest of the week off?"

So I managed to get the week off and then hung up.

"*That's* it . . ."

"What?"

"That's it, right there."

Finally I twigged that Aloha was pointing at the phone.

"Now that looks like something you don't need."

"What? You mean my phone?"

"Right! Let's get rid of it."

Aloha laughed.

"So how about it? One day of life in exchange for your phone."

If phones disappeared from the world . . .

What would I gain, and what would I lose?

Just as my imagination was kicking into overdrive, Aloha came in uncomfortably close.

"So, what are you going to do?"

I weighed it up.

One day of life, or the phone. Mmmm, I wonder . . .

"Use it or lose it!"

"J . . . just a minute!"

"OK, you've got twenty seconds . . . Now ten seconds, nine, eight, seven . . ."

"OK, can you cut it out with the mission control thing? Just go ahead and make it disappear! Get rid of it!"

It was just hard to be convinced I was doing the right thing, not that I was in a position to be dithering.

My life or my phone. Obviously, I'll take life.

"OK! Here we go!"

The Devil sounded like he was having a good time, as usual.

Then I suddenly remembered. I hadn't got around to calling my father in a while.

Oh well. That's just the way it goes, I guess. I hadn't called my father since Mom died four years ago. And I hadn't been to see him either. I heard he was still running the little clock-repair shop in the old neighborhood not far from where I live now, but I never thought of visiting. Not even once. But I admit, it is kind of odd not bothering to drop your own father a line, even when you expect to die soon.

I don't know if Aloha sensed my ambivalence or what, but he came over with that big grin of his.

"There, there, I understand. It's the same with everyone. When it comes to actually erasing things from your life, you start to think. That's why I always include a special offer."

"Offer?"

"Yup. You have the right to use the thing you're about to erase one last time."

"I see."

"So you're allowed to make one last phone call. You can call anyone you want."

That only made me more confused.

Of course, the first person who came to mind was my father. But when I pictured his face, I couldn't help remembering what happened four years ago. And now that it's been like this for so long, what would we have to talk about? I just couldn't call him.

So who will it be? Who gets my last phone call?

Maybe a close friend like K.?

He was definitely a great guy, and if only we could find the time to hang out again after all these years, I'm sure we would still get along great. But on the other hand, we never had any deep and meaningful, or serious conversations. How would K. react if I suddenly called him to tell him that I'm dying, and that my phone is about to disappear, which is why I thought it would be best to call him now? He'd think I'd lost it. He'd assume it was a joke and the call would be wasted. Not the way to use your last phone call.

Back to the drawing board.

So how about a close friend at work like W.?

He was always easygoing and helped me out a lot. He was a bit older than me, always willing to give me some advice, whether it was work-related or general life advice.

He was like my work big brother. But I don't know . . . it's the middle of the working day and all . . . I don't really want to bother him.

The fact that I'm worrying about bothering W. with no warning gives me the feeling that maybe it's a different sort of person I should be using my last phone call on earth to get in touch with. Thinking about it, W. and I never really talked about anything important. When I was drunk and having a good time out with the guys I work with (I get drunk on just one beer so I'm a cheap date) I might have thought we were really confiding in each other, but when you really get down to it, we weren't. We both might have thought that we were talking about the stuff that mattered, but in the end, I don't think either of us gave away all that much.

So there I was, absolutely screwed and approaching the bitter end.

I scrolled through my phone's list of contacts as fast as I could. Names of friends and acquaintances appeared and then disappeared one after the other. Each of the names seemed to carry a hidden meaning. Countless people who I seemed to have had some kind of a relationship with, but when push came to shove, didn't really share much with after all. My contacts list was filled with people like that.

My life was over and I had no one who mattered enough for me to call. I had lived alongside people and created so many links, but they were ultimately all so tenuous. It's really depressing—too depressing—to realize something like that at the end of your life.

I wasn't keen to talk to Aloha about how I was feeling, so I left the room and went and sat on the stairs. I held on to my phone tightly, and suddenly a number began to float up from the back of my brain. It was her number. Somehow I had forgotten it, but it was as if it had been etched on my body. Her number wasn't even in my contacts list. Slowly I began to dial . . .

I finished the call after a few minutes and went back into the room. Aloha was playing with the cat. Actually it was more like a tussle, with both of them rolling and tumbling around on the floor. Aloha seemed to have completely forgotten about me, so I watched in silence for a while.

Minutes went by, then . . .

"Oh! You're back."

Finally Aloha became aware of my cold stare and, somewhat embarrassed, pulled himself up off the floor. He turned to face me, taking pains to put on a serious face.

"Are you done?"

Oh come, on! You're telling me the Devil likes cats? No use acting all cool and pretending nothing happened!

I didn't say anything, but I took a good swipe at him in my mind. When I finally got over it I answered him calmly:

"Yes, quite finished."

"OK, let's go. Make that phone disappear!"

Aloha looked delighted and gave me a wink (kind of a pathetic wink since he didn't seem to be able to close just one eye at a time).

Suddenly the phone, which had been in my hand just a minute ago, was nowhere to be seen.

"All right. Done. See ya tomorrow."

When I looked up the Devil was gone.

"Miaow."

The cat's meow echoed sadly in the apartment.

I had to go and see her—the person I had just phoned. Her.

But then, just as this thought passed through my brain I fell into a deep sleep.

And so my seven-day odyssey had begun.

TUESDAY: IF PHONES
DISAPPEARED FROM
THE WORLD

My roommate is a cat.

You know that old story by Soseki Natsume, *I am a Cat*? It's something like that, but not quite. The cat's name is Cabbage.

You might have forgotten all about this by now, so why don't I try and jog your memory.

I was five when my mother found the abandoned kitten and brought it home with her. It poured with rain that day, and the kitten had been left in a cardboard box by the side of the road. Mom found it on her way home from the supermarket. The poor thing was soaked. Printed on the side of the box were the words "Nagano Lettuce," and so after my mother had got the kitten home and dried it off with a towel she announced, "This little boy's name is Lettuce."

This was pretty unusual—my mother had never liked animals. It took her a while to get used to stroking Lettuce, and at first, she was a bit clumsy. So in the early days, I helped her to take care of the cat, until she got used to him.

To make matters worse, Mom found out that she was allergic to cats. The sneezing just wouldn't stop. For a whole month the tears and sniffling went on and on, but she never considered giving the cat away.

"I can't let him go—he chose me."

Then she'd wipe her flushed, puffy face and carry on caring for the cat.

And then one day, about a month later, Mom's cat allergy suddenly disappeared. It was a miracle, or maybe her body got used to it. In any case, one day it was suddenly gone, and Mom was free of all the symptoms—the sneezes, the tears, and the runny nose.

I remember that day really clearly—Lettuce wouldn't leave her side for a minute, constantly snuggling up to her.

★

"In order to gain something you have to lose something."

Mom said it was just obvious. People are always trying to get something for nothing. But that's just theft. If you've gained something it means that someone, somewhere, has lost something. Even happiness is built on someone else's misfortune. Mom often told me this, she considered it one of the laws of the universe.

Lettuce lived for eleven years. He developed a tumor and lost a ton of weight. Toward the end he just slept a lot, and died peacefully in his sleep.

The day after Lettuce died, Mom wouldn't move. She had always been bright and cheerful, and actually liked cooking and cleaning. But now suddenly she was no longer in the mood to do anything. She just stayed at home and cried. So I did the laundry, and then I'd drag Mom out for dinner at the local chain restaurant. Over time, I think we tried out every item on the menu.

A month went by like that and then one day, suddenly and unexpectedly, Mom arrived home with another rescued kitten in her arms, as if it happened every day.

The kitten looked just like Lettuce. It was a round, black and white mass with a mixture of grey. A beautiful cat. It looked so much like Lettuce we decided to call him Cabbage.

Looking at him all curled up Mom laughed and said, "He really does look just like Lettuce." It was the first time she had smiled in a month. Seeing her laugh again after such a long time made me teary.

Or maybe just well up a bit. I guess I was worried that Mom might just fade away, disappear off to some faraway place and never come back.

Then four years ago she really did leave us.

"What a coincidence—I have the thing that Lettuce had," said Mom, laughing faintly.

Just like Lettuce, the weight dropped off Mom, and in the end, she went to sleep and simply never woke up. She died peacefully.

"Take care of Cabbage," she implored me before she died.

Fate, it seems, has a sense of humor—I'll end up dying before Cabbage just like Mom. She'd be pretty unimpressed with me, I'm sure. I can just imagine her saying she should have left Cabbage with someone else.

*

Next thing I knew it was morning.

For the first time in a while I'd dreamed about my mother.

Cabbage meowed nearby. I pulled him close to me and gave the soft furry ball a squeeze. His silky, fluffy, and warm body was life-giving.

And then I remembered. I had gained one extra day of life.

I was wondering how many of the previous day's events I'd imagined. Maybe it all really happened, but on the other hand, it could have been a dream. But my phone, which I normally would have left on the bedside table, was nowhere to be found. And the fever, which I'd had for so long, had gone, along with my headache. Maybe that meant that the deal I made with the Devil was also real?

Telephones had disappeared from the world.

When you think about it that's not such a bad thing, especially when it comes to mobile phones!

Lately it seemed like I was messing around on my stupid phone all the time, from morning till night, just before bed. I didn't read many books anymore, and I didn't read newspapers. DVDs I borrowed just piled up in my room unwatched.

On the train on the way to work I was always looking at my phone. Even when I was watching a movie, I checked my phone regularly. And when I was eating. When my lunch break came around I got this terrible urge to look at my phone. Even when I was with Cabbage I'd end up looking at the phone instead of playing with him. Being such a slave to it made me hate myself.

Mobile phones have been around for only about twenty years, but in just that short time they've managed to take complete control over us. In just twenty short years something that we don't really need has come to rule our lives, making us believe that we can't do without it. When human beings invented the mobile phone, they also invented the anxiety of not having one.

But who knows, maybe we went through the same thing when people first started sending letters. It's the same with the internet. Throughout human history we've given birth to new things, only to lose the old. When you put it like that, maybe God was on to something when he accepted the Devil's proposal.

*

I know you're probably wondering who I made my last call to.

It's kind of personal, but all right, I'll tell you.

She's the first woman I ever loved. My first girlfriend.

OK, now don't go calling me a sentimental moron.

They say that when a man is dying, the first name that comes to mind is his first love. In this, I think I share something with the common man.

Lounging in the morning sun, I took my time getting out of bed. I listened to the radio while I cooked breakfast. Made some coffee, fried an egg, and plopped one slice of bread in the toaster. Then I sliced a tomato and placed it on the plate. After breakfast I had another cup of coffee and leisurely read a book. Ah, life without a phone. It was so good! It seemed as if time had suddenly lengthened, while the space opened up and spread out.

Midday approached.

I slammed the book shut and headed for the bathroom. I took a nice hot shower, and then put on my clothes (the usual black & white) which lay neatly folded nearby. Then I headed out to see her.

The first place I went after leaving the apartment was the barbershop (my usual place). I realized it was absurd taking the time to get a haircut when I was about to die, but I wanted to look good for my ex-girlfriend, so don't laugh.

After fixing my hair I stopped by the optician's across the street to get new glasses, then went to catch the tram. One was just arriving as I got there so I ran and jumped onto one of its green carriages.

It was a weekday so it was packed. Normally, all of the passengers would be looking at their phones. But today was different. Instead, people were reading books, listening to music, or staring outside at the scenery. People seemed to have no trouble finding something to fill their free time. Their facial expressions seemed cheerful, somehow.

Why do people look so serious when they're checking their phones? It seemed so calm inside the tram without those contraptions. Not only had I won an extra day of life for myself, it looked like I'd also done the world a big favor.

But had phones really disappeared from this world completely?

I looked out the window of the tram at a sign for a noodle shop, which sat on the corner of the shopping district. (This is where Cabbage secretly goes at night for dried bonito shavings.) The shop's phone number appeared on the sign as always. And when I looked around the inside of the tram I could see that there were still posters advertising mobile phones. But no one on the tram was on their phone . . . What did this all mean?

Then I suddenly remembered. Something similar happened in an old comic book series I used to read as a kid. *Doraemon*, Tentomushi Comics, Vol. 4. That's the time one of Doraemon's secret gadgets, the pebble hat, is introduced.

The story goes like this:

As usual, Nobita Nobi (the kid who's the main character in the series) has been told off by his parents. Nobita goes to Doraemon for comfort, complaining, "They don't need to watch me so carefully all the time. I just want to be left alone." Then Doraemon pulls a gadget out of that fourth-dimensional pocket of his: the Pebble Hat.

Doraemon explains: "When you wear this hat, you'll be like a pebble on the ground—unnoticed." In other words, you'll still exist, but no one will notice.

Nobita is thrilled and puts on the hat. For a while, he enjoys being left alone. But then, he starts to get lonely. And when he tries to take off the hat he can't. It's stuck on his head, so he starts to cry. It's his tears that make the hat come off, and Mama and Papa start to notice him again. Then Nobita says, "I'm glad people care about me," and that's the end of the story.

Well, I went off on quite a tangent there, but to get back to what I was saying, I guessed that the system Aloha had made worked something like Doraemon's Pebble Hat. In other words, phones hadn't really disappeared from the world. It's just that nobody noticed them anymore. People had fallen into a collective trance. The Devil was in fact "pulling a Doraemon."

As the long months and years go by, phones will gradually cease to exist completely. Like pebbles on the roadside, they will start by going unnoticed—until they disappear completely.

When you think about it, the 107 people who met Aloha before me must have made something disappear, but the thing is, the rest of us haven't noticed. It's as if without you realizing it, things you use in your everyday life, like your favorite coffee cup or the new socks you just bought, could disappear. And if you did realize, however much you looked for them, you wouldn't be able to find them. For all we know, there may be all kinds of things that have already disappeared without our having noticed it, things that we'd assumed would always be around.

The green tram climbed two hills and finally reached the town next door. The station I got off at opened out onto a large square. From there I headed for where we'd arranged to meet.

At the center of the square stood a clock tower. We used to meet here when we were in college. There was a roundabout that circled the clock tower, and nearby lots of restaurants, bookshops, and those old shops that sell odds and ends.

I was fifteen minutes early. Normally I would have checked my phone at this point, but instead I pulled a small paperback out of my pocket and began to read as I waited for her to get there.

The time came, but she didn't show up. Then half an hour went by and she still hadn't arrived.

Damn.

Without thinking I put my hand in my pocket in search of my phone. It wasn't there. Phones had disappeared from the world.

Had I gotten the place wrong? Or were we supposed to meet at a different time? I started to despair—all of the information I needed was in the phone I'd been using when I made the deal with the Devil. There was a good chance I'd got the time wrong.

"Damn. What a pain in the ass," I muttered out loud.

I was supposed to have been liberated from my phone, but as it turned out, I needed it after all. There was nothing I could do. So I just stood there shivering under the clock tower.

Come to think of it, back then I often found myself muttering the same words. That was back when I was going out with her in college. She was from the big city, but came to this small town out in the sticks to go to college. She was majoring in philosophy. I remember the house where she lived all alone, the electric fan and the small space heater. And all the books. She had lots of books. Even in those days everyone had a mobile phone, that's how we got in touch with each other and communicated—everyone except her. She didn't even have a landline at the house she rented. When she called me it was always from a pay phone.

Whenever I saw the words "telephone booth" light up on the screen of my mobile phone, I would be beside myself with happiness. I would always pick up quickly and talk to her no matter where I was—in class or at my part-time job.

The worst part was when I missed a call. All I could do was stare helplessly at the incoming call history. I couldn't even call back because it had come from a public phone. I had nightmares about empty telephone boxes where the phone rang forever and no one ever answered.

After a while, I started sleeping with my phone, holding it tight against me so I wouldn't miss a call from her. The warmth of the phone I held close to me in bed reminded me of the warmth of her body. I always slept deeply that way.

After we had been seeing each other for about six months, I finally managed to convince her to get a landline installed at her house. So she hooked up one of those old vintage rotary phones in classic black.

"I got it for free!" she bragged to me as she demonstrated the dialing action, which made a loud sound.

I called that old phone so many times the number was seared into my brain. It was like it became part of me.

It's strange how that works. Out of all the numbers stored in my mobile phone I never memorized even one. I can't remember the numbers of close friends or colleagues, or even my parents. I had left the work of memory and even my ties to other human beings to my mobile phone. I no longer bothered to memorize anything. When you think about it, mobile phones have done something pretty scary to the human brain.

Yesterday as I was sat on the stairs, I tried to think of any number that my memory had held on to tightly enough for it to have become part of me, a physical part of me. Naturally it was her number that came to me. It seems that in the end, I had instinctively relied on my own memory.

It had been seven years since we broke up, but there was still something I needed to ask her.

She answered the phone—I couldn't believe she actually still had the same number. She was working at a movie theater in her hometown and the next day just happened to be her day off. I thanked God for this coincidence, and arranged to meet her.

"OK. See you tomorrow."

Her voice hadn't changed at all since we were in college. I felt as if I'd gone back in time.

I waited for an hour below the clock tower until my feet got so cold I thought they had become a part of the pavement. Then she finally arrived, marching toward me.

She hadn't changed a bit. How she dressed, her walk . . . it was all the same. The only thing that was different was that she had cut her shoulder-length hair and now wore it short.

She noticed how pale my face was and seemed worried.

"What's wrong? Are you OK?"

It was kind of disappointing being asked if I was OK instead of something like "how've you been" or "long time no see," having not seen each other for such a long time. We talked a bit and it turned out that I had arrived an hour early. When I said, "Damn. What a pain in the ass," she replied, "Oh really? Why?"

"I'm probably going to die soon."

I told her about my predicament in a nearby cafe.

She remained silent for a while, sipping leisurely on her cocoa. Then looking up at me she said,

"Is that so?"

This took me by surprise. Her response seemed a little glib to say the least.

I had imagined three possible responses. In order of preference they go like this:

"Why? What happened?"

"Is there anything I can do? Just say it. I'll do anything."

Remain silent for a moment and then burst into tears.

Her reaction left something to be desired.

On the other hand, when I think about it, even I acted pretty calm when I was told I didn't have long to live. The whole thing seemed kind of surreal, even to me, so why should I be surprised if other people don't seem shocked, disappointed, or sad.

I wonder why people always expect things from others that they themselves can't or won't do. Did I want her to be shocked, or sad?

"But why so sudden?"

"I just found out. It's cancer."

"Oh, that's terrible . . . but you don't seem upset at all. So I guess people are actually pretty calm when they hear that they might die soon?"

Of course, I couldn't exactly tell her that the Devil was helping me to buy more time. I don't think there's anyone who would want his first love to think he's lost his mind when he's on the brink of death. And besides, that wasn't what I came to speak to her about.

"And so . . ."

"What?"

"Since I might die soon, I feel the need to find out more about myself . . . you know . . . to reach some kind of understanding."

"Is that so?"

"I mean . . . I guess I need to know if my life had any meaning."

"Yeah, I guess you'd wonder about that . . ."

"Well, yeah. So that's why I wanted to talk about us. I mean, our history. I remember all sorts of things about us, but I wanted to ask you what you remember, even the little things."

I realized I'd been talking very fast, and then discovering that my coffee had gone cold, I downed the rest of it in one go.

She didn't seem pleased. "Well, if that was the case you should have given me some advance warning." She stopped and looked deep in thought. Suddenly I felt really awkward, so I went to the bathroom and took my time getting back to my seat.

"Now that's something I do remember."

"What?"

"You always went to the bathroom a lot."

This was her first offering.

"And you always took a really long time . . . for a man."

What? So that was it? No warm up—straight to it.

And besides, she'd never mentioned it before. But now that I think about it, I do go pretty often and take quite a long time. That's because I tend to start thinking about things while I'm in the bathroom, to the point where I sort of drift off. Then I take a long time washing my hands afterward, and walking back from the bathroom and so on. It seemed like *she* hardly ever went to the bathroom. And whenever we used public toilets at the same time, she'd always be out first and waiting for me.

"Oh, and you always sighed a lot. I was always thinking how awful life must be for you."

"Was it really like that . . . ?"

"And you weren't much of a drinker. Couldn't take your liquor."

"Jeez, sorry . . ."

"Oh, yeah, and whenever we went to a restaurant you could never decide what to order . . . even though you're supposed to be a man. And then you'd always end up ordering the same thing anyway—curry rice. And whenever I got angry you'd sulk and take a really long time to get over it."

After blurting all of this out she looked pretty pleased with herself and went back to casually sipping her cocoa.

Wow. So this is what I have to listen to as I approach the end? Did my life have any meaning? Was it worth the effort?

This seemed pretty harsh. So this is what you remember about the man you once loved? Or maybe it's not so strange. Women are always unforgiving and unsentimental about men in their past. That must be it. At least that's what I told myself.

"Oh, right, and one more thing. Whenever you phoned you'd talk a lot, but then when we met in person, like this, you didn't have much to say."

I'll have to admit she was probably right there.

In those days, we'd talk on the phone for two or three hours at a time. And we only lived a thirty-minute walk from each other. Every now and again we'd talk on the phone for eight hours straight, and then we'd laugh, saying if we were going to talk for that long we should have just spent the day together.

But then when we actually did spend time with each other, we didn't seem to have much to talk about. On the phone, it seemed more intimate, even though we weren't with each other, and we'd have the most involved conversations over even the small things.

Even so, her judgment of me seemed a bit negative. Don't I deserve more than that now, when the end is near? I kept on going even though my heart was breaking.

"But then, you did stick around for more than three years, you put up with all of that."

"You can say that for sure! But . . ."

"But what?"

"I liked your phone calls. You used to talk so passionately about music and novels . . . it was as if the world had suddenly transformed. I liked you. I might have even loved you. Even though you were incapable of talking about anything when we actually met."

"Yeah. You're right, you know. The phone calls. It was the same for me. I remember how you'd talk about movies, and how the whole world seemed to change just listening to your voice."

This seemed to break the ice, and we rambled on endlessly after that. Mostly we talked about old times and people we knew back then, like the skinny kid who had now grown incredibly fat, or that girl who was a plain Jane and really stern, but who married right out of college and now had four children.

The next thing we knew it had got dark, so I walked her home. She lived in a little room above the movie theater where she worked.

"So you finally did it—you married the movies."

She laughed at me. "Now, now, you're not allowed to joke about that kind of thing."

★

"So how's your father?" she asked me as we strolled along the cobbled street.

"Mmmm . . . I wouldn't know . . ."

"Still haven't made up?"

"I haven't seen him since my mother died."

"Your mother always said she wanted the two of you to get along."

"I guess we just weren't able to live up to her expectations."

After we had been seeing each other for about six months I took her home to meet my parents. My father didn't even come out of his shop to say hello, but my mother really took to her. Mom served cake and then cooked a meal, and then served more cake after that. She wouldn't let her go home!

"I always wanted a daughter," my mother told her. Mom had only brothers and no sister. Even the cats, Lettuce and Cabbage, were male.

After that the two of them used to go out together without my knowing.

"Your mother was very special," she said smiling.

"What do you mean?"

"When a new restaurant opened she'd get all excited and invite me to go out with her. She taught me how to cook. We'd even go to the beauty salon together."

"Huh? You went to the beauty salon together? I never knew."

Mom died three years after we broke up, but my girlfriend still came to the funeral. She shook and cried, and held on to Cabbage until it was all over. I think she'd sensed how confused and upset Cabbage was, as he went pacing back and forth through the house.

After we broke up Mom would always say, "Now, she was a good catch that one," making sure to slip it in every time I saw her. When I saw how my girlfriend held Cabbage at the funeral, I think I finally understood what Mom had meant.

"How's Cabbage?"

"He's doing fine."

"But what are you going to do about him? Who'll take care of him when you die?"

"I'm thinking about it. I'll find someone."

"Well, let me know if you can't find anyone."

"Thanks."

At the foot of the steep hill we were making our way down I could see the movie theater's sign all lit up. Years had gone by since I last saw the place and now it seemed so small. I first saw it as a student and it seemed big, and colorful. It was the same with the clock tower in the square. The neighborhood remained for the most part unchanged. The real-estate office, restaurants, the prep school, and the flower shop. The only difference was that the supermarket had been done up. But now the town I used to know felt like a miniature model, as if it had shrunk in size. Or was it that the way I saw things had become bigger?

"You know, there was something I wanted to ask you . . ." I trailed off.

"What?"

"Why do you think we broke up?"

"What made you want to know all of a sudden?"

"I guess there must have been some specific reason, but I can't seem to remember now."

Actually, I had been planning to ask her about this the whole time. About why we broke up. Maybe we just got bored, or our feelings got worn out, but I couldn't for the life of me remember what it was exactly that finally drove us apart.

"So do you remember?"

For a while she didn't respond, and then, turning to face me suddenly, fired off a series of questions.

"OK, what's my favorite food?"

What a random question. The seconds ticked by.

"Ummmm, let me think. Is it deep-fried shrimp?"

"Wrong! It's corn tempura!"

Hey, but I was close. They're both fried foods. But wait a minute, what was she getting at with all this?

"OK then, what's my favorite animal?"

"What? Ummm, let's see now . . ."

"Japanese monkey."

Right, right . . .

"Then what's my favorite drink?"

What *was* it? I had no memory of it at all.

"Sorry . . . I give up."

"Cocoa. What I was drinking back there at the cafe. You've forgotten already?"

Right. Now I remembered. She loved corn tempura and always ordered it when corn was in season. She used to say it was her favorite food in the whole wide world. And when we went to the zoo she'd never stray far from the monkey enclosure. And she'd drink hot cocoa all the time, even in summer.

It's not as if I'd forgotten completely. I just couldn't remember at that precise moment. I suppose after we broke up I had just shut away all my memories of her.

Somewhere I heard that people forget in order to build memories. You have to forget in order to move on.

But on the other hand, I'd started to think . . . Now I was staring death in the face, I'd found myself remembering lots of trivial things.

"I guess people forget. It's more or less what I expected. It's the same with us breaking up. It's just one of those things. It's not worth trying to remember all the details."

"Was that it . . . really?"

"Well, if you really want to know, I'd say that that trip we took before graduation was the beginning of the end."

"You mean . . . Buenos Aires? Wow, that takes me back."

All of the dates we went on took place right in the confines of the small town—we never went further afield. We just did laps around town, as if we were playing an endless game of Monopoly. And yet we were never bored.

We'd meet at the library after class and go to a movie. And then we'd go to our usual cafe and talk. Later we'd go to her place and have sex. Every once in a while she'd pack lunch for us and we'd take the cable car to the spot with the best view in town and have a picnic. It wasn't much, but we were happy. It was all we needed.

Thinking about it now it's kind of hard to believe,

but I suppose the size of this town was just right for us then.

We went out for over three years, and we only went abroad once. Argentina . . . Buenos Aires. It was both our first and last trip together.

At the time, we were both crazy about a film by a Hong Kong director, set in Buenos Aires.

So for our last long holiday as students we decided to go there.

We booked a flight on a cheap American airline with a connection part way through. We were permanently cold and the food was awful. After twenty-six hours of travel we finally arrived in Buenos Aires.

From Ezeiza International Airport we took a seedy cab to El Centro. We checked into the hotel and headed straight to our room, to bed, but we couldn't sleep. It didn't matter how tired we were, our inner clocks were still on Japan time. We were on the other side of the world, as well as in a different hemisphere.

So we decided to go out and explore the city.

The beautiful sound of someone playing the *bandoneón* echoed through the streets and dancers did the tango on the cobblestones. The sky hung low in Buenos Aires as we took in the sights. We headed for the famous old Recoleta Cemetery and wandered around its labyrinthine passages, eventually finding the grave of Eva Peron. Later we ate lunch in a cafe while listening to tango melodies played by an elderly white-haired guitarist.

Later in the day we boarded a bus for La Boca, the old working-class district everyone talks about with its colorful houses, street musicians, and other attractions. The journey took half an hour as the bus wound its way through the series of narrow streets. Then the colors of the neighborhood came into view—the wooden houses painted sky blue and mustard yellow, emerald green and salmon pink. As we strolled around, the colors of the houses glowed in the setting sun, as if we were looking at dolls' houses. When night fell, we went to watch a tango show at La Ventana in San Telmo—the heat of the dance took us to another world.

We spent a couple of days strolling through the city, slightly drunk on the passion that hung in the air. Then we met Tom, who was staying at the same cheap hotel as us.

He called himself Tom, but he was actually Japanese. He was a young man of twenty-nine and had quit his job at a media company to travel around the world. In the evenings, we'd go along with him to the local supermarket, to buy wine, meat, and cheese, which we took back to the hotel and ate in the dining room. Night after night we talked until late as we ate and sipped our wine.

Tom told us stories from his travels. He told us about the sacred cows in India, little boy Buddhist monks of Tibet, the Blue Mosque in Istanbul, and the white nights of Helsinki. He told us of seeing the ocean stretch on endlessly in Lisbon.

Tom didn't hold back on the Argentine red wine and was soon stinking drunk, but he could still go on talking.

"There are so many cruel things in the world, but there are also just as many beautiful things."

For us, after life in a small town doing the same thing day after day, it was all so new and fascinating . . . it was impossible to picture the things he described. But even so, Tom had no trouble relating to us, sometimes laughing, sometimes with tears in his eyes. There we were, the three of us on the other side of the world, talking on and on.

Then finally it was almost time for us to return to Japan, but Tom had suddenly disappeared. He hadn't turned up at the hotel after heading out for a day of sightseeing, as usual. We drank wine as we always did and waited for him, but he never came.

The next day we found out that Tom was dead. He had taken a trip to the border between Argentina and Chile to see a historical site with a statue of Christ, and the bus he was on drove off a cliff.

It was like a dream. It didn't feel real. I could still see Tom coming into the dining room with a bottle of wine in one hand saying, "C'mon, time for a drink," but now Tom wasn't coming back. We spent the day feeling stunned.

On our last day we visited Iguazu Falls, making the thirty-minute journey from the nearest airport. We walked two hours until we got to the narrow crack in the earth's surface that they call the Devil's Throat. We'd seen it in the Hong Kong film that made us want to visit Argentina in the first place. It sits at the top of the largest waterfall in the world.

Water rushed over the falls with such an unimaginable force . . . the magnificence of that place, its scale, it gave me a sense of the sheer violence nature is capable of.

Then I noticed that my girlfriend was crying next to me. She raised her voice and screamed and cried, and no matter how loudly she yelled, her voice was drowned out by the deafening sound of the falls.

It was then that it hit me. The real, tangible feeling that someone had died, of having lost someone you'd grown close to. Tom was dead. We would never see him again. No more talking late into the night, drinking red wine, and enjoying meals together . . . It was the first time the reality of death had really hit home for either of us. And so she started to cry there, in that place, where it was so obvious just how powerless, how utterly helpless, human beings are. She went on crying and I couldn't do anything about it. I didn't know what to say. All I could do was stare blankly at the white, foamy water as it came down the falls and was swallowed up by the great hole in the earth.

We left Buenos Aires and returned to Japan via the same route. Again, it took ages. For the whole twenty-six hours that it took to get home, we never spoke one word to each other.

Had we talked too much while we were in Buenos Aires? No, that's not what it was. We could just no longer find the words. It wasn't that we wouldn't talk. We just couldn't. We sat there right next to each other and couldn't explain what we were thinking or feeling. We couldn't speak. We were both in pain because a friend had died, but now we were at a loss for words.

And as we sat there in silence for twenty-six hours

I think we both realized that was the end. I mean, of us. We were so very over.

How strange. We had both felt like we were meant to be together, and both of us had seen the end coming.

I couldn't take the long hours of silence so I started to read back through the travel guide. There were photographs of a massive mountain range. There was Mt. Aconcagua located on the border between Argentina and Chile, the highest peak in South America. I turned the page and there was the figure of Christ the Redeemer of the Andes on top of a mountain, towering over the surrounding area. I wondered if Tom ever made it there, or whether he died before getting a chance to see it.

I imagined Tom getting off the bus and gazing at the beautiful earth spread out below the mountain peaks. As he turns around he notices the huge shadow of the cross and looks up to see the figure of Christ, arms open in a welcoming gesture. The sun hangs in the sky behind the statue at shoulder height, silhouetting it brightly against the clear sky, and Tom squints as he stares up at this vision of light.

I began to well up. It was too much so I turned to look out of the window of the plane. Outside I could see the ocean filled with icebergs stretching on and on into the distance. The setting sun gave the endless sea of ice a purple hue—it was so beautiful it was almost cruel.

Twenty-six hours later we were back in our little Monopoly town.

"OK, see you tomorrow."

She shouted over her shoulder as she got off at her station and headed down the steep hill just as she always did. I saw her off, silently watching the figure with perfect posture move gradually into the distance.

A week later we broke up. One short five-minute phone call and it was done. Just like that. It was like filling out a change-of-address form or something at the local council office. A short, businesslike conversation and it was all over. Over time we had clocked up more than a thousand hours in telephone conversations, and now all it took was five minutes to end the relationship that had been the basis of it all.

The telephone made it easy for us to get in touch quickly, but in exchange, we missed out on the chance to get to know each other in a profound way, to become truly close. The phone did away with the time needed to develop real feelings and memories, and finally what feelings there were just evaporated.

My phone bill, which arrived without fail each month, would list a total of more than twenty hours' worth of calls, with a charge of 12,000 yen. I don't remember us ever talking about whether the cost of talking on the phone was worth it. I wonder how much I was paying per word.

We could talk all we wanted over the phone, but that still didn't guarantee that we'd really have a deeper connection. And then, when we stepped out of the Monopoly game we'd been playing around our little college town, and into the real world, we found out that the old rules—the only things that made our relationship possible in that particular time and place—no longer applied.

In any case, the romance between us had been over for a while. For some reason we'd carried on playing anyway, following all the rules. All it took was a few days in Buenos Aires to make it obvious to us that those rules had become meaningless.

But one small morsel of pain remained. Just one little regret. And that is the feeling that if we had just had our phones with us on that flight back to Japan, maybe, just maybe we could have talked about our feelings and wouldn't have had to break up. Monopoly was over, but maybe we could have tried a new game.

This is how I pictured it:

We're on the plane and God brings us telephones. So I call her (even though she's sitting right by me) and start to speak.

So what are you thinking about?

You go first.

I'm sad.

Me too.

I was thinking about you.

I was thinking about you too.

So what are we going to do?

I don't know. What should we do?

I just want to go home.

Yeah, me too.

So what shall we do next?

I don't know.

Why don't we move in together?

That might be a good idea.

We can have coffee at home.

And cocoa.

If only we'd had telephones with us then . . .

We could have talked on the phone during the whole flight back to Japan. Not about anything special, necessarily—just talking would have been enough, so the other would know someone cared. It would have been nice to have taken the time to listen to what the other was feeling. If only . . .

I still remember the faint smile she gave me when we said goodbye at the station near her house. That smile became a small wound that opened somewhere in the back of my brain. It acted up on rainy days like an old football injury.

But when I think about it, I guess it's not that unusual. I mean, I must have a whole collection of small injuries, tucked away somewhere in the back of my memory. I suppose that's what some people call regret.

"Um, so about today . . ."

The sound of her voice suddenly brought me back to the here and now. I realized that we'd arrived at the movie theater where she lived.

"Yeah?"

"I'm sorry I said a lot of mean things to you."

"Oh, no big deal. It was interesting."

"But you remember, right, we made a promise?"

"Huh?"

As usual I had forgotten what she said.

"Don't you remember? We promised that if we ever broke up we'd say what we didn't like about each other."

That's right. We had made a deal. We promised that we'd admit all the things we didn't like about each other if we ever broke up. We thought that way we'd learn something about love, about being in a relationship. The lover is the eternal teacher. I'm pretty sure I used those exact words (without any irony!). At the time, she said she couldn't imagine ever breaking up with me. I felt the same way.

"So I told you everything I didn't like about you. Just so you'd know before you die."

She was clearly enjoying this—she let out a little laugh.

"Thanks for keeping your promise. Even though it's not exactly what I want to hear when I'm on the brink of death."

I laughed too.

When we began our relationship, I just couldn't imagine it would ever end. I just assumed that because I was happy she must be happy too. But a time came when that was no longer the case. Feelings can't always be mutual.

Love has to end. That's all. And even though everyone knows it they still fall in love.

I guess it's the same with life. We all know it has to end someday, but even so we act as if we're going to live forever. Like love, life is beautiful *because* it has to end.

★

"You're going to die pretty soon, right?" she said, opening the large, heavy doors of the movie theater.

"You make it sound like it's no big deal."

"Well, I was just thinking I could do a screening of your favorite film for you, one last time, if you know what I mean?"

"Wow, thanks."

"OK, be back here at nine tomorrow night. It'll be an after-hours showing. Bring a film that you love."

"Will do."

"Oh, and before you go, I do have one question."

"Not again!"

"What's my favorite place?"

Oh man, what was it? I've forgotten everything.

"OK, so you don't remember, right? Then we'll make that your homework. Come back with the answer tomorrow night."

And with that, she closed the movie theater's large doors.

"See you tomorrow," she mouthed through the glass.

"OK. Tomorrow!" I shouted back.

The street went dark the moment the theater lights were turned off.

I stared at the old brick movie theater for a while,

under the red and green lights of the sign. It had been a strange day.

Phones had disappeared from the world, but what had I lost?

I had trusted this device with my memory and my relationships, and when it suddenly disappeared, the anxiety was overwhelming. More than anything, it was really inconvenient. I felt so lonely and helpless waiting under that clock tower—more than I thought I would.

With the invention of mobile phones, the idea of not being able to find the person you're supposed to be meeting disappeared. People forgot what it meant to be kept waiting. But the feeling of impatience at not being able to get hold of her, the warm feeling of hope, and the shivering cold were all still fresh in my mind.

Then suddenly I remembered—of course. That's it. Her favorite place. This is her favorite place. Right here. The movie theater!

That's what she'd always say back then.

She felt as if there'd always be space for her, a seat just for her, at this movie theater. As if her being there made the place complete.

That's what she always told me.

Now I knew the right answer, I had to tell her

right away. My hand dived into my pocket to grab my phone. But of course, damn! It wasn't there. No more phones . . .

This was so annoying. I really wanted to let her know right away. I looked back at the theater as I made my way slowly back up the street. Then I remembered what it was like when I was a student and I'd wait for her to call. It felt the same way now. I wanted to let her know what I was thinking right away, but couldn't. And strangely enough, it was when I couldn't speak to her that she was on my mind the most.

In the old days before mobile phones and email it would have been a letter. People would imagine their letters reaching their loved one and wonder how they'd react. Then they would eagerly wait for a letter in reply, checking the mailbox each day. Presents are like that too. It's not the thing itself, but what it might mean to the person you give it to, and it's their expression and how happy they'll be to receive it that you have in mind when you pick the gift.

"In order to gain something you have to lose something."

That's what Mom always said. I remember, that was the day the sneezing suddenly stopped. She was stroking

Lettuce, who was curled up on her lap, and said it with such conviction.

I thought about my girlfriend as I looked up at the theater sign, and I began to feel her words weighing down on me.

"I mean, you're going to die pretty soon, right?"

Suddenly I felt a sharp pain in the right side of my head. My chest was tight and it felt like I couldn't breathe. I felt so cold I began to shiver, my teeth chattering.

So I guess I'm going to die after all.

No, I don't want to die.

I couldn't hold myself up any longer and fell to my knees in front of the movie theater. Suddenly I heard my own voice behind me.

"I don't want to die!!!"

I turned around in surprise.

It was Aloha.

"Got ya, didn't I? Man, should've seen the look on your face!"

There stood Aloha in the subzero temperature wearing his trademark Hawaiian shirt and shorts, sunglasses perched on top of his head. Where there had been palm trees and American cars, he now sported a shirt printed with dolphins and surfboards.

What a b— Try putting on some clothes, will you. I was so pissed off, but I couldn't afford to get angry.

"So, dude, you got a date. Hey, I'm jealous. I've been watching from the sidelines all day. Looked like you were having a great time."

"Wait, you were watching us the whole time? Where were you?" I asked, breaking out into a cold sweat.

"Up there." Aloha pointed with his finger up at the sky.

I couldn't handle this guy anymore.

"But anyway, seriously, you don't want to die yet, right? You're getting to be pretty attached to life."

"I guess . . ."

"Oh, there's no doubt about it, you don't want to die! It's the same with everyone."

It was embarrassing, but I had to admit it. Or to be fair, it's not that I didn't want to die, it's just that I couldn't take the fear of facing death, of approaching the end.

"So anyway, time for your next step. I've decided what you're giving up next."

"What?"

"This!"

Aloha pointed at the movie theater.

"So how about it? We get rid of movies in exchange for your life."

"Movies . . . ?" I said under my breath, gazing up at the movie theater, my vision getting fuzzier.

I think of all the times I went to the movies with my girlfriend, and the endless films we saw together. Various scenes float before my eyes: a crown, a horse, clowns, a spaceship, and a silk hat, a machine gun, the vision of a naked woman . . .

Anything can happen in the movies: clowns laugh, spaceships dance, and horses talk.

I must be having a nightmare.

"Help!"

I called out, but could barely hear my own voice. I passed out then and there.

WEDNESDAY: IF MOVIES
DISAPPEARED FROM
THE WORLD

In my dream the man says, "Life is a tragedy when seen in close-up, but a comedy in long-shot." The little tramp wears a silk hat and an oversized suit, twirling his walking stick as he approaches. I've always been moved by these words. When I first heard them and even more so now. I want to tell him how important they are to me but I can't get the words out.

The little man continues: "There's something just as inevitable as death. And that's life."

Yes, I get it! For the first time I understand the significance of these words, now that I'm so close to death. Life and death have the same weight. My problem is just that for me the scales are starting to tip more toward the latter.

Until now I'd been living as best I could, and I don't think I was doing too badly. But now, all I seem to have left is regrets. It feels like my life is gradually being crushed by the overwhelming weight of death.

The man in the suit seems to know what I'm thinking and comes over, stroking his little toothbrush mustache. "What do you want meaning for? Life is desire, not meaning. Life is a beautiful, magnificent thing, even to a jellyfish."

That must be it. It has to be. Life has meaning for everything, even a jellyfish or a pebble by the side of the road. Even your appendix must exist for a reason.

So what does it mean when I make something disappear from the world? Isn't that an unforgivable crime? With the meaning of my own life so up in the air, I'm beginning to wonder whether I might actually be worth less than a jellyfish.

The funny little man in the suit comes even closer. Now I recognize him. It's Charlie Chaplin. He stands there right before my eyes and holds his hat in front of his face. He makes a sound like a meow, and when I look again I see a cat wearing a top hat. I tried to cry out again, but still couldn't make a sound. The next thing I knew I was leaping out of bed.

I looked at my watch. It was 9:00 in the morning.

Cabbage was looking at me with a worried expression. He meowed and then curled up by the pillow. I stroked him gently. So soft and warm, and fluffy-feeling . . . *This* was what life felt like.

Finally the cogs in my brain started to turn again, and gradually the events of the previous night came back to me. I had collapsed in front of the movie theater after coming over all cold and dizzy. But after that was a total blank. My head still hurt a bit and I had a slight fever.

"OK, OK, c'mon now, what is this? Don't be such a drama queen!"

I was calling from the kitchen. I mean, not me, but my Devil doppelgänger.

"Oh, give me a break. It's only a cold!"

"What do you mean, only a cold?"

Aloha's red shirt was so gaudy it hurt my eyes.

"I'm saying, it was just a cold and I had to drag you all the way back here. That's hard work, dude, even for a devil!"

Aloha poured some hot water into a mug, added honey and lemon, and began stirring.

"You seemed to be suffering so much I thought you were going to die."

Aloha brought over the mug and plonked it down beside me.

"Well, sorry . . ."

I sipped the sweet and sour liquid. It was delicious.

"Just so you know, this life-prolonging treatment has always worked out for me in the past. Always. We've come this far. If I mess up, God will be angry with me, OK?"

"I'll be more careful in the future . . ."

"You're not exactly in a position to be talking about the future, OK? You just remember that!"

There was always something with Aloha. But there was nothing much I could do about it. The guy was throwing me a lifeline.

"Miaaa . . ." Cabbage let out an exasperated meow and then got up and left. Apparently even he'd had enough.

"So, what are you going to do?"

Aloha waited for me to finish the honey-lemon and then resumed giving me the third degree.

"About what?"

"Oh, c'mon now . . . we're talking about what you're going to make disappear from the world next."

"Oh, right . . ."

"Next it's movies."

"Sure."

"Do we go ahead? Press the delete button, or would you rather quit right here?"

If movies disappeared from the world . . .

I tried to imagine what it would be like.

It wouldn't be easy. I'd lose my main hobby.

OK, so I realize it was a bit late in the day to be waxing lyrical about hobbies (I mean with the whole death thing and all), but I'd bought so many DVDs . . . what a waste. And I just bought new box sets of Stanley Kubrick and *Star Wars*.

Mmmm . . . did it have to be this way? I guess my life depended on it. Literally.

"Hurry up, hurry up!" Aloha was pressing for an answer. But this was a serious problem. I needed to think a minute.

"So does it have to be movies?"

"Yes."

"There's no other way?"

"Well, let's see . . . shall we try something else?"

So how about music?

NO MUSIC, NO LIFE.

Can't live without music!, as the sign outside my local Tower Records store said.

Would it be possible to live in a world without music?

I suppose we'd all manage somehow.

All those rainy days holed up in my room listening to Chopin . . . I guess I could do without it. It might still be the same. There'd be other things to find comfort in. But what would a sunny day be like without Bob Marley . . . ? Not quite the same, but I guess I'd manage.

The almost unbearable high I get from listening to the Beatles while speeding along on my bike. It's my background music at work, while I'm delivering the mail. But I guess I'd get by.

And then listening to Bill Evans on the way walking home in the dark . . . giving that up would be painful, but I guess I'd manage without it.

Conclusion 1:

NO MUSIC, YES LIFE.

I'd go on living even without music, though it'd be sad.

NO COFFEE, NO LIFE! NO COMICS, NO LIFE!

OK, just thought I'd throw these in for comparison. Let's say there's no more coffee or comics. Life would go on. I'm sure I could live without Starbucks caffè lattes. And comics? It would be hard, but I could do without *AKIRA*, *Doraemon*, or *Slam Dunk* if it meant my life.

Look, I'll level with you. I didn't want to give up

anything, definitely not my collection of anime figures or my limited-edition trainers, but it's the same as, say, getting rid of hats, or Pepsi, or Häagen-Dazs ice-cream. I wouldn't like it, but it's not like I'd die without them. I'd give them all up in a second in exchange for my life.

So I'd tried giving up everything (only in my imagination, for practice).

Conclusion 2:

Basically, all human beings *really* need to survive is food, water, and shelter.

In other words, pretty much everything in this world, everything in the human world that humans made, is pretty unnecessary—OK to have around, but we could do without.

I've had a thing for movies my whole life. So the question is, if all movies disappeared, would it feel like part of me had gone too?

"There is a difference between knowing the path and walking the path."

That's a line from *The Matrix*.

It seems to me that the idea of something disappearing from the world and what that would really be like are two totally different things. It's not only about something suddenly not being there—there's something else that can't be measured. It's a real loss, something deeply human, that can't be expressed by counting things. It's so small you could miss it, but without anyone noticing, our lives are changed completely.

More than anything it made my heart ache. My girlfriend who loves movies so much, everyone around the world who loves movies . . . if I robbed all of these people of something that matters so much to them, I'd be committing a crime. And that kind of guilt would be a heavy thing to carry around.

But then again, what about my own existence? It was either me, or movies. Ultimately my life—which was now hanging by a thread—was non-negotiable. If I was dead, I wouldn't be able to enjoy movies anymore, and I wouldn't be able to appreciate my girlfriend's love of movies, or how much they mean to so many people.

So I made a decision. Make movies disappear.

The main character in a movie I saw put it this way:

"There are lots of people in this world who want to sell their souls to the devil. The problem is, there isn't a devil around who's willing to buy."

But actually they got it wrong. In my case, a devil who wanted to buy my soul really did appear before me. Obviously I never dreamed the Devil himself would ever *actually* appear.

"So, it looks like you've made your decision."

He seemed pretty cheerful, at least Aloha—who I could only assume was the real Devil—was grinning as he spoke.

"Yes . . ."

"OK. You know the rules. You get to see one last film—just one now. Take your pick."

Right. I got to choose one last film. But there're so many! It was too much for me. I couldn't choose.

"I'll give you one last showing of your favorite film right here. I'll even watch it with you."

I remembered my girlfriend's parting words from last night. It's almost as if she knew what was coming.

Anyway, out of all the movies I loved, I had to pick which one would be the last I ever saw. That's not an easy thing to do. Should I choose from all the films I've seen before, or something I haven't seen yet?

I had read magazine articles and seen TV shows where someone is faced with a question like what would you have for your last meal, or what would you take with you to a desert island, but I never imagined that someday I'd be faced with the same kind of choice. It felt impossible. But in my case, turning Aloha down wasn't really an option. I mean, it was do or die.

"Can't decide, huh? I get it . . . and I'm not surprised. You really *do* like movies, don't you?"

"I really do . . ."

"Well, if that's the case, I'll give you half a day to decide. The last movie of your life!"

I was at a complete loss, so I decided to visit Tsutaya. Yes, I know it's the name of a store, but it's also the name of a guy I know.

OK, I know that's weird.

Let me explain.

I was at a complete loss, so I decided to visit the local video-rental store, which, by the way, is not a Tsutaya store. The guy who works there is an old friend of mine from junior high. He's like a regular walking encyclopedia when it comes to movies, so we gave him the nickname Tsutaya. I decided to visit him, and get some help with making my decision.

Tsutaya had worked in the rental shop for over ten years. When you add it up, he's probably spent half his life there—and he's spent the other half watching movies. To put it bluntly, other than when he's asleep, his entire life is devoted to movies. He's made of movies. The biggest movie geek on earth.

Tsutaya and I met each other in spring, the year we both started junior high and were in the same class.

For the first two weeks of school Tsutaya just sat alone in the corner and spoke to no one, not during class or at recess. So I went over and talked to him, and we became close friends, just like that.

I don't remember what made me finally break the silence. I guess I believe that this happens maybe three times, tops, in someone's life—that you meet and are attracted to someone whose personality is so very different from your own. Either you become lovers (which would happen, in my case, if the person was a woman) or you become best friends.

There was something about Tsutaya that really drew me to him. So I just started talking to him and we became close friends.

But even when we'd grown really close, Tsutaya didn't talk much, and he was too shy to look you in the eye. Our eyes can't have met more than two or three times. But I liked him anyway. Normally he wouldn't say much at all, but if we talked about movies, suddenly the words would start pouring out of his mouth, he'd get a glint in his eyes, and he'd just go on and on. I realized then that when a person talks about something they really love there's a kind of thrill to it.

In junior high I learned a lot about movies from Tsutaya, and I watched everything he recommended. He knew about all kinds of films, from Japanese samurai movies to Hollywood science fiction and French New Wave, and even Asian indie films. His movie geek-dom knew no bounds.

"What's good is good," Tsutaya would always say.

He was unsurpassed in his knowledge of movie trivia. He could tell you what genre the film belonged to, when it was made and where, the cast and the director. It didn't matter what era or nationality you were talking about. It was all the same to him. Ultimately, "what's good is good" was all that mattered.

As luck would have it, we were also in the same class in high school. So in effect, I got six years of private tutoring in film studies for free. I'd say that I was now an expert. But compared to Tsutaya, I realize that most people who claim to be experts in film are just fakes (I'd probably have to include myself in that bracket). In this day and age, when people lay claim to expert status without having done more than dipped a toe in the subject, Tsutaya was the real thing. He was an authentic, natural-born geek. Hardcore. Although that didn't necessarily mean I wanted to be just like him. I mean, all geeky and stuff (no offense, of course).

★

It was an eight-minute walk to the video-rental shop.

As usual, Tsutaya was there behind the counter. He had become so fixed in that one position over the years, he looked like a statue of a sitting Buddha on the altar of a temple. When viewed from the outside, it was more like the shop and the infinite number of DVDs had grown up around him, with Tsutaya fixed in the middle.

"Tsutaya!"

I called his name as I passed through the automatic doors of the shop.

"H-hey, l-long time no see. W-w-what's wrong?"

Not quite Buddha . . . Tsutaya still couldn't look you in the eye, even as an adult.

"Look, I know this is out of the blue, but I don't have any time to chat."

"W-w-what's wrong?"

"I've got terminal cancer. I'm going to die soon."

"Huh?"

"I could die tomorrow."

"Wha-whaaat?"

"So I have to decide what the last film I see before I die is going to be, and I have to decide quickly."

"H-how?"

"Tsutaya, I need your help. Can you help me decide what to watch?"

I could tell by Tsutaya's expression that being given such a responsibility out of the blue had left him at a bit of a loss.

Sorry, Tsutaya. I realize this is all quite sudden.

"R-really?"

"Yes, really. It's a shame, but that's the way it goes."

Tsutaya screwed his eyes shut. He looked like he might be grief-stricken, or maybe just trying to think. He let out a deep breath and opened his eyes. He got up from behind the counter and wandered through the maze of shelves.

Tsutaya had always been that way. If someone needed help, he got to work quickly and did whatever was needed without asking why.

We both scanned the shelves full of DVDs and Blu-rays. A never-ending succession of movies passed before my eyes. Realizing this would be the last time I ever watched a film, I found myself remembering scene after scene, line after line from my favorites.

"*Everything* that *happens* in life can *happen in a show*."

So sings Jack Buchanan in *The Bandwagon*.

But really, could everything that had happened to me lately happen in a movie?

One day I'm diagnosed with terminal cancer—with

no warning—and told I don't have long left, then the Devil himself appears, wearing a Hawaiian shirt, promising to make things disappear from the world one by one in exchange for granting me one more day of life. It just doesn't work. It's too fantastical. Life is stranger than fiction!

Tsutaya was wandering around the section devoted to Westerns.

"With great power comes great responsibility."

Peter Parker reminds himself in *Spiderman*, having developed super-powers.

Maybe it was the same for me. I had been making things disappear from the world in exchange for my life. Which was a pretty big responsibility, as well as a risk, and a stressful dilemma to have. Come to think of it, having signed on the dotted line with the Devil, I was beginning to understand just what Spiderman must have gone through.

What should I do? I was none the wiser, but maybe movies could offer some moral support.

"May the Force be with you!"

Thank you, *Star Wars*, and to you, the Jedi knights.

"I'll be back."

The Terminator, I know how you feel—I want to come back too!

"I'm the king of the world!"

Oh, DiCaprio. Come on, man, calm down.

"Life Is Beautiful!"

Now, that is a load of rubbish!

Suddenly a voice from behind me . . .

"Don't think! Feel!"

I'd become completely absorbed by my own miserable thoughts when suddenly Tsutaya turned to me and spoke. In his hands he held a copy of *Enter the Dragon*.

"D-d-d-don't think! Feel!"

Tsutaya cried out again.

"Thank you, Tsutaya. Bruce Lee's great, but somehow it doesn't seem like a good candidate for the last movie you want to watch just before you die."

I laughed at his suggestion.

"When I buy a new book, I read the last page first. That way, in case I die before I finish, I know how it ends."

So says Billy Crystal in *When Harry Met Sally*.

Standing there looking at the shelves just made it impossible to ignore the fact that I was going to die before I had the chance to see them all. I couldn't help but think of all the movies I hadn't seen, all the meals I hadn't eaten, and all the music I hadn't heard.

When you think about it, it's the future you'll never get to see that you regret missing the most when you die. I realize it's strange to use the word "regret" about things that haven't happened yet, but I couldn't help thinking something along the lines of "if only I would be alive." It's a strange idea. Although really, when it comes down to it, none of these things matter, in the end—like all the movies I was about to make disappear completely.

Eventually we ended up at the shelf that held Chaplin's entire back catalog.

I found I was whispering to myself:

"Life is a tragedy when seen in close-up, but a comedy in long-shot."

The dream I'd had earlier that morning came back to me.

"Th-th-that's from *L-Limelight*, right?" Tsutaya missed nothing.

In *Limelight*, the little tramp, played by Charlie Chaplin, tries to stop a ballet dancer, whose hopes have been dashed, from committing suicide. He tells the dancer:

"Life is a beautiful, magnificent thing, even to a jellyfish."

He was right, even jellyfish are here for a reason— they have meaning. And if that's the case, then movies and music, coffee and pretty much everything else must have some kind of meaning, too. Once you start down that path, then even all those "unnecessary things" turn out to be important for some reason or another. If you're trying to separate out the countless "meaningless things" in the world from everything else, you'll eventually have to make a judgment about human beings, about our existence. In my case, I suppose it's all the movies I've seen, and the memories I have of them that give my life meaning. They've made me who I am.

To live means: to cry and shout, to love, to do silly things, to feel sadness and joy, to even experience horrible, frightening things . . . and to laugh. Beautiful songs, beautiful scenery, feeling nauseous, people singing, planes flying across the sky, the thundering hooves of horses, mouth-watering pancakes, the endless darkness of space, cowboys firing their pistols at dawn . . .

And next to all the movies that play on a loop inside me, sit the images of friends, lovers, the family, who were with me when I watched them. Then there are the countless films that I've recorded in my own imagination—the memories that run through my head, which are so beautiful, they bring tears to my eyes.

I've been stringing together the movies I've seen like rosary beads—all human hope and disappointment is held together by a thread. It doesn't take much to see that all life's coincidences eventually add up to one big inevitability.

"S-s-s-so, I guess that's all, right?"

Tsutaya put *Limelight* in a bag and handed it to me.

"Thanks."

"Um, I d-d-don't know what's going to happen now, but . . ."

Tsutaya started to choke up and couldn't get any more out.

"What's wrong?"

Tsutaya hung his head and began to cry. He cried like a baby, tears flowing down his cheeks.

I was reminded of when Tsutaya would sit on the window ledge at school and look so lonely. But as I watched him sitting on his own there by the window, it actually felt like I was drawing strength from him. He would never do anything other than what felt most important to him—and he had no problem doing it alone, at his own speed, without needing validation from the people around him. Seeing him there, just doing his thing, just being himself, somehow made me feel like things would be OK. At that point in my life, nothing was really that important to me. Looking back, it wasn't him who needed me. It was really me who needed him.

All the feelings I'd been bottling up suddenly came pouring out and I began to cry too.

"Thank you."

I managed somehow to get the words out.

"I-I j-just want you to stay alive," Tsutaya said between sobs.

"Don't cry, Tsutaya. It's not all that bad. I've got a good story and someone to tell it to. You remember what they said in *The Legend of 1900*. And right now, Tsutaya, that's what you mean to me. It's because you're here that I'm not completely done for."

"Th-thank you."

Having said the words, Tsutaya just stood there and carried on crying.

"So how'd it go? Did you decide?"

I'd made it to the movie theater at last, where my girlfriend was waiting.

"Well, this is it."

I handed her the package.

"*Limelight*, eh? Interesting . . . Good choice."

She opened the DVD box and then looked a little stunned. There was no disc inside. The packet was empty.

98

The store always rented out DVDs in their boxes, so every once in a while there would be a screw-up like this. But how about that for timing!

Tsutaya, this is a pretty crucial error!

On the other hand, as Forrest Gump said, "Life is like a box of chocolates. You never know what you're gonna get."

So true! You never know what you're gonna get. It's pretty much the story of my life! Life is a tragedy when seen in close-up, but a comedy in long-shot.

"What do you want to do? We've got a few films on hand here."

I thought for a moment and then came to a conclusion. If we're being honest, I'd reached it quite some time ago.

What's the last film you'd want to watch? The answer was quite simple, really.

I walked into the theater and sat down.

Fourth row from the back, third seat from the right. This was our spot all through our college years.

"OK. Roll 'em!"

Her voice rings out from the projection room. The show begins. Light is projected onto the screen. But there's nothing there but a blank space, a rectangle of white light illuminating the screen.

I had chosen nothing.

As I gazed at the blank screen I remembered a photograph I once saw. It was a picture of the inside of a movie theater. It was taken from the projection room and showed the seats and the screen. The photograph captured one entire film, and was taken by opening the shutter at the beginning of the film, and then closing it when the film ended. In other words, the photograph recorded one entire two-hour-long film. The result of absorbing the light from every scene in the movie was that the picture shows nothing but a white rectangle.

I suppose you could say that my life is like that photograph. A movie that shows my whole life, the comedy and the tragedy. But if you put that all into one still photo, all that would be left is a blank screen. All the joy, anger, and sorrow I've been through, and the result is that my life shows up as nothing more than a blank movie screen. There's nothing there, nothing left. Only an empty blank space.

Sometimes, when you rewatch a film after a long time, it makes a totally different impression than it did the first time you saw it. Of course, the movie hasn't changed.

It's you that's changed, and seeing the same film again makes that impossible to forget.

If my life were a film, it would have to find a way of showing my changing perspective. That's to say, how I see my own life has changed over time. I would feel affection for scenes that I'd hated before, and laugh during scenes where I'd originally cried. The past love interest is now long forgotten.

What I'm remembering now are all the good times I had with my mother and father. Only the good times . . .

When I was three years old, my parents took me to the movies for the first time. We saw *E.T.* It was pitch black inside the theater, and the sound was so loud. The theater was filled with the buttery salty smell of popcorn.

On my right sat my father, and on my left was my mother. Sandwiched between my parents in the dark theater, I couldn't have escaped even if I'd wanted to. I just looked up at the huge screen and watched. But I remember almost nothing about the movie.

The only thing I remember is that scene where the boy, Elliott, rides through the sky with E.T. on his bike. It's a powerful memory. It made me want to shout, or cry, or something . . . It seems to me that that's what movies are all about. I can still remember the impression it made on me—it was overwhelming. I held on tight to my father's hand and he held mine tightly in return.

A few years ago a digitally re-mastered version of *E.T.* was showing on late-night television. I hate watching movies on TV, with the constant interruptions from adverts, so was about to turn it off, but once I started watching I was gripped.

About twenty-five years had gone by since I first saw the film, but I still found myself as moved by the same scenes as I had been as a child. I couldn't stop myself from crying. But that still doesn't mean that the experience was exactly the same as it had been when I was three.

For one thing, twenty-five years later I knew I'd never fly through the air like they do in the movie. And it's been years since I spoke to my father, who back then was sitting next to me holding my hand tightly. Meanwhile, my mother, who sat on my left in the theater, is no longer of this world. So I suppose I know two things I didn't know then. I can't fly, and what I had then has gone forever.

What did I gain by growing up, and what did I lose? I can never resurrect the thoughts and feelings I had in the past. When I think about that, I feel a wave of sadness so strong that the tears won't stop.

Sitting alone in the movie theater staring at the blank screen I started to think.

If my life were a movie, what kind of a movie would it be? Would it be a comedy, a thriller, or maybe more of a drama? Whatever it would be, it definitely wouldn't be a romantic comedy!

Toward the end of his life, Charlie Chaplin said something along the lines of:

"I may not have been able to produce a masterpiece, but I made people laugh. That can't be all that bad, can it?"

And Fellini said:

"Talking about dreams is like talking about movies, since the cinema uses the language of dreams."

They created masterpieces, made people laugh, gave them dreams and memories.

But the more I thought about it, the more I realized that my life just didn't lend itself to being adapted for the big screen.

As I stared at the blank screen, I tried to imagine what it would be like.

I am the director.

Then there is the film crew and the cast, made up of my family, friends, and former lovers.

The opening scene is set thirty years ago, when I am born. There is my infant self and my parents smiling down at me. Relatives gather around and all take turns holding the new baby, squeezing its hands and pinching its cheeks. Soon the new baby learns to turn over, crawl, then stand up on its own, and before you know it begins to walk. Subject to all the same hopes and fears of all new parents, my mother and father take to their roles with gusto, feeding, clothing, and frantically playing with the baby.

Is it possible to imagine a healthier and more normal start in life? Our opening scene couldn't be happier.

Then, as anger, tears, and laughter flit across the screen, I gradually grow up. I talk less and less to my father. Who knows why, after all the time we'd spent together? I've never figured it out.

Then one day a cat arrives in our home. Its name is Lettuce. There are lots of happy times, between Mom, Lettuce, and me. But Lettuce eventually grows old and dies. And then my mother dies. Cut to the most tragic scene in the film.

So Cabbage and I are left behind. We decide to go on living together. My father is out of the picture at this point. I start working as a postman, and normal everyday life goes on.

Could this be more boring! Scene after scene of mundane detail, line after line of trivial dialogue. What a low-budget movie! And on top of all that, the star of the show (me!) doesn't show any sign of having a goal in life, or values of any kind. He's an apathetic guy, completely without any spirit, who is of no interest at all to the audience.

Obviously the film would never work if it showed my life exactly as it is. The script would have to be written in a hyper-real, in-your-face kind of style, with more of a sense of theater. A dramatization. Sets can be simple, pared back, but they'd have to have a certain flavor to them. Props are picked out to add to the sense of atmosphere, and costumes would come in black and white.

And what about editing? The scenes are all pretty boring so they'll need some fairly major editing. But if it goes too far we'll only be left with like five minutes of film. That's no good. It would be a good idea to start by taking a careful look back through the script. Completely unnecessary scenes run way too long. And the scenes we really want to see are cut right at the point where they're getting good. But that's pretty much what my life has been like.

And what about the soundtrack? Let's see, maybe a nice melody played on piano, or on the other hand perhaps something grand and stately, with a full orchestra? No, let's try something more relaxed, like an acoustic guitar. But whatever we go for, I have only one request— that during the sad scenes, up-beat music should play in the background.

Now work on the film is done. It's a quiet, low-key production, and probably won't be a box-office hit. Its release will be pretty subdued, and it's likely to go mostly unnoticed. It will probably be the kind of film that goes to video quickly, and is left in a corner of the rental shop, the colors on its box fading.

The last scene ends and the screen goes dark. Then the credits roll.

If my life were a movie, I'd want it to be memorable, in a way, no matter how modest the production was. I'd hope it would mean something to someone, somehow, that it would give them a boost and spur them on.

After the credits, life goes on. My hope is that my life would go on in someone's memory.

The two-hour screening ends.

I step outside the theater and the quiet and the darkness envelops me.

"Do you feel sad?" she said, as we left the theater.

"I don't know."

"I guess it must be rough on you."

"I don't know. Sorry, I really don't know how I feel right now."

And I really didn't know. I wasn't sure if I was sad because I was going to die or if I was sad because something really important and meaningful was about to disappear from the world.

"You can come back and see me any time, you know, if you ever feel bad, if you're in so much pain you can't stand it."

Her words reached me just as I was about to turn away.

"Thanks," I said, and headed back up the hill.

"Wait!"

She shouted from behind me.

"One more quiz!"

"Not again . . ."

"This is the last question. Just one more."

As she shouted after me I could see she'd begun to cry. Then seeing her cry made me feel like crying.

"OK. I'll give it one last go."

"Whenever I watch a movie with a sad ending I always watch it one more time. Do you know why?"

This time I knew the answer. It's the one thing I remembered well.

It's something I was hoping for during the whole plane ride back from Buenos Aires, and even for a while after we broke up.

"Yeah, I know."

"OK, so what's the answer?"

"Because you're hoping that maybe it'll have a happy ending the next time."

"Right! That's it!"

She wiped her eyes roughly with her sleeve, and giving me a big wave, shouted manically, "May the Force be with you!"

To which I responded, holding back the tears, "I'll be back!"

When I got home Aloha was waiting for me sporting a big grin. He gave me a wink (of course he can't really wink so it's more like kind of a squint), and with that, made movies disappear.

While Aloha was busy erasing movies, I was thinking about my mother. There was an Italian movie she liked a lot. Fellini's *La Strada*.

The story goes like this: Gelsomina, a naive young woman, is bought from her impoverished mother by brutish circus strongman Zampanò, who wants her for his wife and partner. She remains loyal despite the abuse she suffers at Zampanò's hands as they travel the Italian countryside performing together. Eventually Gelsomina grows weaker and when the abuse becomes intolerable, she begins to physically waste away. Zampanò abandons her.

A few years later the traveling circus arrives in a seaside town and Zampanò hears a young woman singing a song that Gelsomina used to sing. Zampanò finds out that Gelsomina has died, but her song lives on. Listening to the young woman singing Gelsomina's song, Zampanò realizes that he loved her. He walks to the shore and collapses in tears on the beach. Crying won't bring her back. In the end he realizes that although he really did love her, he was incapable of treating her as if he did, when they were together.

"You only realize what the really important things are when you've lost them."

That's what my mother would say when she watched this film.

It seemed like the same thing was happening with me now. I was genuinely sad now that I'd actually lost movies. I knew I would miss them. I know it was stupid, but it was only when I realized that the movies were really gone that it hit me how much they'd helped me emotionally, and how much they'd had to do with making me who I was. But my life was more important . . .

The Devil picked that moment to announce in his usual cheerful manner the next item he'd make disappear.

I couldn't think about anything anymore, so I said yes just like that.

At that point, the thought that it could happen to Cabbage had never crossed my mind.

THURSDAY: IF CLOCKS
DISAPPEARED FROM
THE WORLD

It's funny how one strange thing is often followed by another. Like when you lose your keys and you invariably end up losing your wallet. Or in a baseball game when your team hits one home run after another. Or how a whole series of major manga artists just happened to end up living in the same cheap apartment building (the Tokiwa-So) in the early 60s.

As for me, I end up with terminal cancer, the Devil appears, phones and movies disappear from the world, and the next thing I know the cat is talking.

"Why, are you still sleeping, sir?"

I had to be dreaming.

"By George, you will get up this instant!"

It had to be a dream.

"Come now, up with you!"

But no, it wasn't a dream. He was actually talking. And the he who was speaking was definitely Cabbage. And for some reason he sounded so refined . . . It was hard to know exactly what was going on.

"A bit confused, are we?"

Aloha appeared with that big grin on his face. Today he wore a sky-blue Hawaiian shirt. Again I felt like telling him to put on some real clothes. In keeping with the flamboyant style I'd come to expect from him, the brightly colored shirt featured parakeets and huge, swirly lollipops. It was so bright it made my eyes hurt. Not exactly the easiest thing to wake up to. Aloha was getting to be a pain in the ass. I snapped.

"C'mon, man, you're always doing this to me! Now I wake up and the cat's not meowing, it's talking. And like a member of the landed gentry! Seriously, what's happening here?"

"My, aren't we witty this morning. Well, that's just a little something extra from me, to you."

"Something extra?"

"That's right. After all, there are no more phones, the movies that you were so attached to are gone, so I thought you might need a little something to cheer you up. Like someone to talk to, or a new hobby or something. So, I just thought I'd try making the cat talk. I just happen to dabble in magic—you didn't know? After all, I *am* the Devil . . ."

"But having the cat suddenly start to talk is a bit, um, disconcerting, I guess. Can you get it to stop?"

"Oh?"

Suddenly Aloha fell silent.

"Did I say something wrong?"

Aloha remained tight-lipped.

"I hope this isn't something that you can't fix—like you can't put things back to normal."

"Well, no, that's not it. I mean, I can put things back . . . or should I say, it'll all go back to normal eventually, it's just a question of timing. You might say . . . I mean, God knows! But anyway, *I* don't really know. I mean, I'm not God, you know? I'm just the Devil."

How about if I just smack your head against the wall! is what I was thinking, but I swallowed my words and burrowed deeper under the covers. A world with no movies and where cats talk was not a world I wanted to wake up in.

Then Cabbage began to walk on my face. He'd always do this to wake me up (I was never a morning person). I once heard that the origin of the Japanese word for cat, "neko," is actually "sleeping child" (same sound, different choice of kanji characters), but I think that's a load of rubbish. Cabbage never sleeps late—he always wakes up early and starts harassing me.

"I shall be most put out if you don't get up soon!"

Cabbage rattled on, letting out a loud moan that sounded distinctly cat-like.

"That's it! I can't take this anymore."

Reality, it seemed, would not leave me alone. I gathered what energy I had and jumped out of bed.

"Oh, and just to check, you do remember, don't you?"

Aloha thrust his face close to mine as he spoke.

"What? What do you mean?"

"What I'm erasing today, of course!"

I had no memory at all of what that was supposed to be. What had he made disappear? What was next on the list? Looking around the room I saw no change.

"Sorry, I don't remember. What was it?"

"Honestly, what am I going to do with you . . . It's clocks, man. Clocks."

"Clocks?"

"That's right. Today you erased clocks."

Ah, now I remember. I made clocks disappear.

*

If clocks disappeared from the world . . .

Would the world change? I thought about it for a while.

The first thing I thought of was my father. I could see him in my mind's eye, hunched over, working in his shop. You see, my father ran a small clock shop.

The ground floor of the house I grew up in was my father's shop. Whenever I went downstairs I would see my father bent over his workbench in the semi-darkness, the desk lamp shining over where he worked, repairing clocks.

I hadn't seen my father in four years. He was probably still repairing clocks in that small shop, tucked away in a corner of that small town.

If clocks were to disappear from the world, there would be no more need for clock-repair shops. No need for that little shop, nor my father's skills. When I thought of it that way I started to feel pretty guilty.

But had clocks really disappeared from the world? It seemed hard to believe that they could all disappear so suddenly. I looked around the room. My wristwatch was definitely gone. And the small alarm clock I had in my room was nowhere to be found. Maybe it was like when phones disappeared—maybe I'd simply stopped seeing them, but whatever had happened, practically speaking, clocks had disappeared from the world.

Then I realized—without clocks, how would I have any sense of time? It looked and felt like morning. And since I had overslept a bit I figured it was probably around 11am. But even when I turned on the TV the time didn't show up on the screen as it usually did, and of course phones had already disappeared, so I couldn't rely on that. If I was being honest, I had no idea what time it was.

And yet I didn't really feel any difference. Why was that? This was different from when I'd made the other things disappear. Other than a few pangs of guilt when I thought of my father, I felt no pain, no sense of loss. But this should have had a pretty huge impact on the world. Clocks make the world go round.

Schools and businesses, public transport, the stock market, and all other public services must be in chaos.

But for someone like me, on my own here (well, plus one cat), there wasn't really much of a difference. It seemed like we were getting along just fine going about our normal lives without clocks, or much of an exact sense of time at all. It didn't really make any difference.

★

"So why are there clocks in the first place?"

I thought Aloha might know.

"That's a good question. But even before clocks were invented, it was only humans that had a sense of time."

"Huh? I don't get it."

Seeing I was puzzled, Aloha went on.

"OK, stay with me. You see, time, or that thing we call time, is simply produced by arbitrarily determined rules. Rules that human beings made up. I'm not saying that the cycle of the sun rising and setting doesn't exist as a natural phenomenon—because obviously it does— but it's humans who have imposed an organizing system on that process and called it time, giving names and numbers to different parts of the day like, say, six o'clock, twelve o'clock, midnight and so on."

"Oooh, riiight . . ."

"So, human beings may think that they're looking at the world as it is, but they've got it all wrong. In actual fact, they've just imposed a meaning on things, come up with a definition of what the world is all about which happens to suit them. And *I* just thought it might be interesting for people to see what the world would be like without that system of telling the time, which humans just made up for their own convenience. You know, just to mix it up a bit . . ."

"Oh, so just like that, huh? Just because you were in the mood?"

"Yeah, well, that's what this is all about, right? So listen, have a great day! Oh, right, there's no such thing as a day anymore!"

And then, Aloha disappeared—his glib parting words still hanging in the air.

The story of the last one hundred years could probably be made to fit onto one page of a history book. Or maybe only a line would do.

When I found out that I didn't have much time left, I decided I'd try thinking of an hour not just as sixty minutes, but 3,600 seconds, just to make myself feel better. But since clocks had now disappeared, counting seconds didn't mean anything anymore.

Even the meaning of words like "today" or "Sunday" had become dubious. But after Wednesday comes Thursday, and since I knew it was morning, that meant that today must be Thursday. Which is not to forget that these days are only arbitrary human inventions . . .

But anyway, I didn't have anything in particular to do, so I thought I'd just kill some time. Although there was no time to kill. And even if I decided to waste time, there was no time to waste either. This really left me with very little to go on.

How many minutes had passed since I woke up? I'd usually glance at the alarm clock by my bed when I woke up, but now there were no clocks. A world without clocks. I was being pulled along in the endless undercurrent of time. I couldn't see it, but I could feel myself being dragged out to who knows where. After a while, it felt as if I was being drawn back into the past.

When you think about it, people sleep, wake up, work, and eat according to the established set of rules we call time. In other words, we set our lives by the clock. Human beings went to the trouble of inventing rules that imposed limits on their lives, boxing them up into hours, days, and years. And then they invented clocks to make time's rule over us even more precise.

And the fact that there are rules means that we've given up some of our freedom. And yet humans have put reminders of that loss of freedom everywhere—hanging clocks on walls, dotting them around their houses. But as if *that* weren't enough, they make sure there's a clock wherever they go, whatever they're doing, by going so far as to wrap them around their wrists. Humans have even felt the need to wrap their bodies up in time.

But now I think I get it.

With freedom comes uncertainty, insecurity, and anxiety.

Human beings exchanged their freedom for the sense of security that comes from living by rules and routines—despite knowing that costs them their freedom.

While I was thinking this over, Cabbage sidled up to me. Usually when Cabbage comes over and shows me any affection it's because he wants something.

"What's wrong, Cabbage? Are you hungry?"

That's usually what he wants in the morning.

"No, that is not at all what I want."

"Oh?"

I was still struggling to believe that the cat was talking back to me. Cabbage let out a deep sigh.

"Sir, you have once again completely failed to understand correctly."

"Sir? What's that all about?"

Apparently he meant me. So how far is he going to take this gentleman thing?

"If you'll permit me to explain. When I want to take a stroll, you think I want to eat. When I do in fact want to eat, you think it is a moment's rest—'a nap' if you will—that I want, and when it is 'a nap' that I require, you believe I wish to play with you. Your judgment is always, if I might say so, just a touch off."

"Oh really? Is that so?"

The cat nodded and continued.

"Yes. It is so. You behave as if you have an understanding of my kind, when in fact you do not understand cats at all. You ask me if I am sad when I am not sad, and see fit to approach me with that purringly sweet voice. I do wish you'd stop that! Oh well, in truth, you're not the only one. All humans are this way."

I was shocked. I had lived with Cabbage for four years and I thought we understood each other. It can be brutal when cats start to speak your language.

"I'm sorry, Cabbage. So what is it you *do* want to do?"

"I would like to go for a walk."

Cabbage had loved taking walks since he was a kitten.

"This cat is just like a dog!" Mom would laugh as she talked about Cabbage. I remember how she would often take him out for walks.

I told Cabbage to give me a minute to get ready, and went to the bathroom. I was mid-way through relieving myself when suddenly I heard the door handle being fiddled with. The door opened and Cabbage barged in.

"Come now, hurry hurry! Let's go."

All right already! I pushed Cabbage out of the bathroom, finished my business, and then washed my hands and face. As I splashed the water around in the sink I could feel Cabbage's eyes on me, pressuring me to go faster. When I looked around I saw him watching me from the shadow of the wall.

"Oh, do come on. I am quite ready for a walk."

"OK, Cabbage, just wait a sec!"

It used to be a meow was enough, but now he was talking to me. This really was making things much more difficult!

I took my clothes off quickly and jumped in the shower. As I was washing my hair I sensed something behind me, like a ghost. It was like being in a horror film—it sent chills down my spine. I kept my eyes closed tightly to keep the suds out until I finished rinsing my hair. When I opened them, I noticed the door was ajar and Cabbage was peering inside.

"Let's go!"

Are you a stalker or something? I felt like shouting, but managed to keep it in. I slammed the door and finished rinsing my hair. I had a simple breakfast, just a banana and some milk, then quickly got dressed.

"Really I must insist. Open the door this instant. I wish to go out."

Cabbage was in the small entry to the apartment scratching at the door with his claws. I was more or less ready, so I caught up with him and we left for a walk.

The weather was good. A perfect day for a walk. Cabbage walked ahead with a spring in his step. Mom would always go out on walks with Cabbage. When I think about it, that means Cabbage got to know a part of my mother that I never saw. In any case, I decided I would take it easy and spend the day with Cabbage.

Another thing I wondered about was how was it that Cabbage came to speak like an upper-class gentleman. Then suddenly I knew.

It was Mom's influence.

Around the time Cabbage first came to live with us as a kitten, Mom suddenly got into TV period dramas. (This was during the "My Boom" of the late 1990s when it seemed like everyone was adopting short-lived obsessive interests.)

She would watch popular long-running series and declare that "all Japanese men should be like this".

Along with her personal "boom" came outdated theories about Japanese masculinity.

"Sorry, Mom, but I really prefer films to TV shows."

I politely refused her offers to join in with her historical drama obsession.

So Mom would watch hours of TV with Cabbage curled up on her lap. Cabbage must have learned human language from the shows they watched.

So Cabbage's Japanese was an odd mixture of my mother's speech and period TV dramas. It was kind of terrible . . . and yet kind of cute too. So I decided I wouldn't try and correct it. This is what was going through my head as I followed behind Cabbage.

Cabbage's preferred route for his walks was overgrown with weeds, but here and there wildflowers also bloomed. Below a telephone pole I noticed some dandelions flowering inconspicuously, and it occurred to me that spring was on its way. Cabbage went up to the flowers and smelled them.

"Dandelions."

When I said the word Cabbage made a face.

"One would call these dandelions?"

"Didn't you know?"

"No."

"It's a flower that blooms in spring."

"Ah, I see . . ."

Cabbage went on to approach every flower we passed along the roadside, asking endlessly, "And what might one call this?", "And this?"

There was an endless variety of wildflowers growing by the side of the road, and Cabbage wanted to know them all: vetch, shepherd's purse, common fleabane, marguerite, Paris daisy, henbit, and so on.

The wildflowers on the roadside were exposed to the north wind and completely dependent on what little warmth they could get from the sun. At that time of year, they were in full bloom. I trawled my memory to try and find the names of the flowers, to teach them to Cabbage. It was strange how the names did come back to me— memories from my childhood, all that time ago.

Like Cabbage, I used to take walks with my mother when I was small. I would ask her questions too: "What do you call that? And that?" I suppose I was just like Cabbage. To think that Mom spent her days like that, putting up with me, and then later putting up with Cabbage.

"You'd find a flower and then sit down, then find another flower and sit down again. Walks would last forever. It's not easy taking care of a small child."

My mother would tell me this, once I'd grown up.

"But those were happy times all the same."

She'd get that faraway look in her eyes, talk nostalgically about the past, then let out a little laugh.

*

125

Having taken our time, Cabbage and I finally reached the park at the top of the hill.

There was a beautiful view from the park. Just below us we could see the road we'd hiked up, lined with houses. Then beyond that was the sea, the color of lapis lazuli. It was a particularly big park, but it had a swing set and slide, and a seesaw for kids. Mothers played with their small children in the sandbox.

Cabbage circled the park, played a bit with the children, and then headed toward the benches where the old men played Japanese chess. "Get out of my way, I'm sitting here," he announced. I was worried that the sudden appearance of a talking cat would frighten the old men, but they just smiled and laughed. Apparently I was the only one who could hear Cabbage speaking.

"No, Cabbage. These people are using the bench now," I said.

But Cabbage was having none of it. Suddenly he jumped up onto the chess board and the pieces went flying. But the old men just laughed it off and acted like it happened all the time. They gave up their spot for Cabbage.

I hung my head apologetically as the old men got up and left. Cabbage gave me a side-glance and positioned himself on the wooden bench, from which ribbons of blue paint were peeling off. He started licking his paws.

It looked like he wasn't going anywhere for a while, so I sat down beside him and gazed absent-mindedly at the ocean that extended for as far as the eye could see. It seemed possible that this peaceful moment might last forever. I looked over at the park's clock tower as I tended to do. As I suspected, there was no clock. Was the disappearance of time responsible for this calm? Or had it always been that way? I couldn't tell. But now that I had finally come to terms with the fact that clocks were no more, I felt light and free.

"Humans are strange creatures."

Cabbage must have finished grooming himself. He looked in my direction as he spoke.

"What's that?"

"Why do humans give flowers names?"

"That's because there are so many different kinds. Without names you wouldn't be able to differentiate between them."

"Just because there are different kinds it doesn't mean you have to name each and every one. Why not just call them all flowers? Isn't that good enough?"

I suppose he was right. Why do people name flowers anyway? And flowers aren't the only thing. We give names to all kinds of objects. Colors have names and so do people. Why do we need names?

It's the same with time. The sun comes up and it goes down. Humans went and imposed their own system of months and years, hours and minutes, on what was a natural phenomenon. Then we gave all those things names. And that's all that time is.

Cabbage existed in a world without time. No clocks, no schedules, and no being late. And no such thing as categorizing people according to age or what year they are in school. And no vacations because there's nothing to have a vacation from in the first place. There's just the changes brought about by natural phenomena, and our physical response—like when you're hungry or sleepy.

In a world with no clocks, I could take my time and think about things. It seemed to me that there were all kinds of rules made up by human beings—rules that begin to fall apart when you look at them closely. I find myself coming to the realization that the ways we have of measuring things—like, say, temperature, or the reflection of light that produces color—are artificial human creations, just like time. Basically humans just applied labels to the things they sensed. From the perspective of the nonhuman world, hours, minutes, and seconds don't exist. Nor do colors like red, yellow, and blue. And temperature doesn't exist. But on the other hand, if yellow and red don't exist, does that mean Cabbage doesn't think dandelions are pretty, or that roses are beautiful?

"But you know, Cabbage, it was really sweet of Mom to go along on those long walks with you."

"How so?"

"Spending all this time with you was a big deal for her. Mom was really fond of you."

"Mom, you say?"

"My mother. I guess she was kind of your mother too."

"Exactly who is this person you refer to as 'mother'?"

I was speechless.

Cabbage must have forgotten about Mom.

But that's impossible. Or on the other hand, maybe he'd made himself forget about her.

I remembered my mother's face the day she rescued Cabbage. She looked a bit sad, and yet she was also so happy. She would watch TV with Cabbage curled up on her lap, stroking him until he fell asleep. Then she would fall asleep too, tucked up with Cabbage on the sofa. She looked so peaceful. I got choked up thinking about it.

"Don't you remember Mother?"

"Who is it you speak of?"

Cabbage had the look of someone who was wondering what the hell I was talking about. He really must have forgotten about her. It suddenly hit me how sad this was. Cabbage's complete innocence just made me feel worse. I guess somewhere deep down I always believed those stories about animals that never forget their master, like in the story of Hachikō, who for years waited at the station for his master to come home, without realizing his master had died . . .

But I wonder if that's just wishful thinking on the part of humans. Would Cabbage forget about me soon, too? Would there come a day when I disappeared from Cabbage's world?

All the moments I'd lived through, more or less without thinking about it, began to feel very important. How many more walks would I be able to take with Cabbage? With the amount of time I had left, how many more times would I be able to listen to my favorite music? To enjoy a cup of coffee, a good meal? To say good morning, sneeze or laugh?

I'd never thought about life this way before. It hadn't crossed my mind during any of my visits to my mother. If I'd realized that someday it would all have to end, I would have appreciated the time I spent with her more. Before I knew it Mom was gone. She died before any of these things had occurred to me.

Had I done anything significant during my thirty-year existence? Had I spent time with the people I really wanted to spend time with? Had I said all that needed to be said to the people who mattered?

There was a time when I could have called my mother, but my mind was always on my mobile's recent call history. I was so busy dealing with what happened to come up at any given moment that I left all the important things for later.

I got so caught up with all the little everyday things that I ended up wasting the time I could have spent on more important things. But the scariest thing is that I never even *noticed* that I was wasting my precious time. If only I'd stopped for a moment to get some perspective, away from all that busy running around. It would have been obvious what the most important thing was, and which of those calls (if any) really mattered.

I looked at Cabbage.

While I'd been thinking, he'd curled up and gone to sleep on the bench. With his four white feet tucked in and folded under his black and grey fur, he looked like a perfectly round throw-pillow. I stroked him and felt his little heart beating away. It was almost unbelievable that such a life force flowed through this small creature, as he lay there so still, sleeping peacefully.

I've heard it said a mammal's heart beats around two billion times during its lifetime. The life expectancy of, for example, an elephant, is about fifty years. For horses it's twenty years, and cats ten years, while a mouse will last only for about two years.

But whatever the average lifespan, all of their hearts beat around two billion times. The average life expectancy of a human being is seventy years. I wondered if my heart had beaten two billion times.

My whole life up to this point, I'd faced what I thought was an infinite tomorrow. But once I discovered that my life would indeed end, it felt more like the future was coming to meet me. Now I found myself heading toward a future that was set in stone. At least, that's how I felt.

How ironic. For the first time in my life I was taking a long hard look at my future, but only after being told that I didn't have long to live.

The right side of my head began to hurt and I was finding it difficult to breathe.

I didn't want to die yet. I wanted to go on living.

So tomorrow I'd once again make something disappear from the world.

Which is to say, something would have to disappear from my future, so that I might live longer.

Cabbage slept on.

The park had emptied of children and the sun had moved further and further toward the west. Cabbage finally woke up. He stretched as far as he could without falling off the bench and let out a great yawn, which he seemed to take his time recovering from. Cabbage stared at me lazily.

"I say, shall we go now?"

Cabbage, still groggy from just having woken up, spoke in a pretty condescending tone, addressing no one in particular. He jumped down from the bench and sauntered off with his usual jaunty stride.

Cabbage headed toward the street that led to the station, through the shopping district. He stopped in front of a soba shop and gave a loud meow. The shop owner emerged with a handful of bonito flakes left over from the day's batch of soup stock, which they served with the noodles. Once he'd polished off his winnings, Cabbage licked his chops and walked off, muttering "excellent" under his breath as he went. With this kind of behavior it was difficult to tell who was the master and who was the pet.

It seemed Cabbage had become quite the local celebrity in the shopping district. Wherever he went, people who knew him shouted hello. It looked like I'd become the retainer of the lofty-speaking cat. Though on the other hand, Cabbage's popularity meant that I was able to buy vegetables and fish and everything else on sale. Who would have thought that there was such a thing as a cat discount!

"From now on I'm always going shopping with you!" I told Cabbage, carrying as many shopping bags as I could in each hand.

"Yes, that's all very well. Now you can make me a meal I actually like."

"That's what I always do. How about that cat food, Neko-Manma, that I always feed you?"

Cabbage skipped a little ahead of me then suddenly stopped in his tracks.

"What's wrong?"

He looked pretty angry.

"Regarding this so-called Neko-Manma . . . there's something I've been wanting to say to you for some time now."

"What? OK, go ahead. Say it."

"Just what is this stuff you call Neko-Manma anyway?"

"Huh?"

"It's just a hodgepodge of table scraps and other questionable material you humans have thrown together and given a pretty name to."

He seemed to be about to burst with frustration and let out a gruff yowl. He went over to a nearby telephone pole and began sharpening his claws by digging them into the wood.

I hadn't realized how much he hated what I'd been feeding him. Again I thought about all the customs we humans have just made up. Just then the little apartment we lived in together appeared in the distance, down the hill from where we were.

After we got home we ate grilled fish together (the real thing), and continued our quiet and relaxing day.

"So, Cabbage . . ."

"What is it?"

"You've really forgotten all about Mom?"

"I don't remember a thing."

"That's so sad."

"How so?"

I didn't know how to explain to Cabbage why it was

sad. And I couldn't blame Cabbage for forgetting either. But at the same time, I wanted to tell him something about the time he spent with Mom . . . I mean, that was real. There was no denying it happened.

I stood up, went over to the closet, and pulled out an old cardboard box. Inside the dust-covered box there was a dark-red photo album. I wanted to show the album to Cabbage.

I turned the pages and explained to Cabbage what was in each photo.

I showed him a photo of the old rocking chair where Mom used to sit with him, rocking back and forth with him on her lap. This is you, Cabbage. This is where you always sat. And this is the ball of yarn you liked so much. You'd play here for hours on end. And here's the worn-out old tin bucket where you used to curl up and go to sleep. I remember you peering out at Mom. And there's that old green towel you liked. It was Mom's favorite, but you adopted it. Then there's the little toy piano that Mom bought you for Christmas. What a picture. Here you are playing on the toy piano. You were a bit rough with it, but what a performance. And then this one, the Christmas tree. I remember when Mom decorated the tree each year you'd get too excited. You'd tear every-thing down as soon as Mom got it up, so she always had a really hard time. Oh, and this one. This is you jumping out at the Christmas tree. What a mess. You were really something, Cabbage. But Mom looks happy in all these photos.

We finished one album then started on another. I kept talking to Cabbage. I told him about Lettuce and that rainy day he came to live with us. How when Lettuce died Mom just sort of shut down. She wouldn't move or go out. Then I told Cabbage about the day she found *him*, and all the happy days that came after that. And I told him about how Mom got sick. Cabbage sat quietly and listened closely to every word.

Every once in a while I'd ask Cabbage if he remembered any of these things, but he seemed to have forgotten everything. Then suddenly, looking at one photo, his eyes lit up.

It was early in the morning at a beautiful spot on the coast. In the picture I'm wearing a yukata, an informal summer kimono. And Mom and Dad are in the photo too. We're pushing Mom in a wheelchair, and on her lap sits Cabbage with a grumpy look on his face. Dad and I are laughing, though looking a bit embarrassed. The laughing faces were unusual and caught my eye.

"Who is this?" Cabbage asked with interest. It was the first time Dad had appeared in any of the pictures.

"That's my father," I answered him curtly. I didn't want to talk about my father.

"Where was this picture taken?"

"I think this was taken at the hot springs we visited together."

There was a date printed on the photo. It was only a week before Mom died.

"Mom was hospitalized and couldn't move around on her own anymore. Then suddenly she said she wanted to go to a hot spring."

"Why was that?"

"I think she probably wanted to leave us with a nice memory. She rarely took trips anywhere."

Cabbage stared intently at the photo.

"Did you remember something?"

"I . . . I think so. I think I'm starting to feel something."

It looked like Cabbage might have recovered a fragment of his memory. I wanted to see if I could get him to retrieve a little more so I carried on showing him photos and talking him through them.

The one from four years ago . . .

Mother's condition had become hopeless. She was throwing up and in pain every day. She couldn't sleep.

But then one morning she woke up and suddenly called me into her room. She said she wanted to go to a hot spring, somewhere where she could see the ocean.

I was bewildered by this sudden request, and asked her again and again if she was sure she wanted to take the trip. I couldn't tell whether she really meant it or not. But Mom really wanted to go. She hadn't made any special requests up to that point, so I was surprised.

I managed to convince the doctor to let her out for just a day or two, but then she revealed her plan.

"I want the whole family to come. You and your father and Cabbage."

That's what mattered to her. To have the whole family together.

Despite my mother's condition, I hadn't exchanged one word with my father during the whole time she'd been ill. I don't think I'd even made eye contact with him. Our relationship, or lack thereof, had hardened over the years. Once we'd established that we never spoke, then that was just the way it was, it had gone on so long. So you can imagine I balked at the idea of going on a trip to a hot spring with him, or even talking to him about it. But I knew that this would be my mother's last trip, so I took a deep breath and decided to see if I could convince my father to come.

"What a stupid idea," my father replied—which was his response to just about everything. But despite my feelings of disgust and the mental exhaustion that came from trying to communicate with him in any way, I persisted and managed to convince him.

It was the last trip my mother ever took. And also the first time I'd ever traveled any significant distance with her, so I went out of my way to put together an especially nice itinerary. It was a three-hour trip by train to a hot spring on the coast. The beach stretched as far as the eye could see, bathed in soft sunlight. It was an elegant inn with a beautiful view of the coastline. My mother had seen the place in a photo in a magazine—it was somewhere she'd always wanted to go.

The inn was perfect—a traditional old farmhouse built over a hundred years ago, remodeled for use as a hotel. There were only two rooms, and a dazzling view of the ocean from the second floor. There was a pretty rustic outside bathing area and beyond that, the coast spread out into the distance. You could sit and watch the sunset. I was sure Mom would be happy with the choice so I put everything I had into getting a reservation there.

So on the appointed day the whole family set out on our trip, with the doctors and nurses waving us off in front of the hospital. It was the first time in a long while that the whole family, all three of us plus the cat, had gone away together.

In the train we sat facing each other in crowded seats, with my father and me barely speaking. Mom was opposite us, just smiling and watching. We survived the three hours spent together in the same communal space, and then just when we were approaching our limit, the train arrived, the conductor loudly announcing the stop for the hot spring.

I pushed my mother in her wheelchair and, feeling hopeful, we headed for the inn.

But when we got there, disaster struck: my reservation hadn't gone through, and someone else had taken the room.

I couldn't believe it. I told them again and again that I had made a booking over the phone. I told them how much this meant to my mother—how it would be her last trip. But they refused to listen to my pleas. The owner expressed her apologies very politely, but wouldn't budge. I was at a loss, and felt devastated that I hadn't been able to do something to make my mother happy.

"Don't worry about it," she said, smiling. But I couldn't forgive myself. I was so frustrated and disappointed I thought I might cry. Not knowing what to do, I just stood there in stunned silence.

Then my father patted me on the shoulder with one of those large, firm hands of his.

"Well, we can't have your mother camping out in her condition. I'll go find something."

Then Dad ran out the door of the inn. I had never seen him move so fast my whole life. So I ran after him.

Dad raced between the nearby inns, checking whether they had any rooms available. Growing up, I only ever saw my father in his shop, sitting silently and still, repairing clocks. I couldn't believe he could move at such speed. Even when he came to watch me play sports at school he would always sit absolutely still, like a rock. This was the first time in my life I'd ever seen him run, for any reason.

"Your father was actually pretty fast on his feet back in the old days."

I remembered what my mother had said as I dashed around, trying to keep up with my father, who despite his compact, muscular frame, ran around the hot-spring resort with surprising grace.

It was high season and all of the inns were full. We ran around trying everywhere, but were turned away time and time again. Some places only one of us would try, others we went to together, pleading with the innkeepers. We just couldn't leave Mom without a decent place to stay. We wanted to make this trip special for her. That was the first time—maybe the only time—since becoming an adult that my father's feelings and my own were in sync.

After scouring the inns lining the beach, running backwards and forwards, we finally found a vacancy. It was dark, and the outside looked a bit shabby. It looked a bit older than the other inns and was a bit rundown. Our first impressions were confirmed when we went inside and the floorboards creaked as we walked up to the front desk.

"It's a pretty good inn," Mother said, beaming, as we brought her in. But I felt awful having her stay in a place like this. But as Dad said, it couldn't be helped—Mom couldn't exactly camp out in her condition. So lacking any alternative, that's where we stayed.

The state of the place may not have been great, but the innkeeper was warm and friendly. The meal wasn't exactly extravagant, but the cook had obviously put his heart into it, and it was delicious. Mom exclaimed over and over again how good it was there, and how good the food was. Seeing her smiling made me feel a bit better.

*

That night we all slept in one big tatami room, our futons lined up all in a row. It was the first time in ten years that we'd been together like that.

Staring up at the old wooden ceiling, I was reminded of the house we lived in when I was in elementary school. It didn't have many rooms, and the entire family slept together upstairs in the only bedroom, futons next to one another.

Now, twenty years later, we found ourselves doing the same thing. It was a strange feeling. And it would be the last time we would ever be together like this. With all these thoughts running through my head, I couldn't sleep. I wonder if Mom and Dad felt the same way. It was quiet, and the only sound I could hear in the small dark room was Cabbage's breathing, blending in with, but just detectable above, the rhythmic sound of the ocean's waves.

Finally it began to get lighter outside. It was maybe four or five in the morning. I got up off my futon, and sat in the window seat. I opened the curtain and looked outside. To my surprise, the old inn sat so close to the beach that the sea occupied most of the view that I saw before me. It had already been dark by the time we found the inn, so I hadn't noticed how close we were.

For a while I sat there and gazed at the ocean,

which—wrapped in pale morning light—looked like something from a dream. Then I noticed that my parents were both awake. They both had circles under their eyes. I guess they hadn't been able to sleep either.

Mother, still wearing her bedtime yukata, looked out the window at the panoramic view of the sea and suggested that we all go for a walk on the beach.

"Let's take some pictures. I love walking on the beach in the morning."

Cabbage was still sleeping, so Mom grabbed him and put him on her lap. She adjusted her yukata and was ready to go. Once she was ready in her wheelchair, off we went to the beach. The early morning light was still dim and it was a bit chilly. Mom wanted to go closer to the water, but it was difficult pushing the wheelchair in the wet sand. After a while I couldn't get it to move at all. Then the sun began to rise, its rays falling on the surface of the ocean creating a sparkling effect. All three of us stopped, captivated by how beautiful the scene was.

"Hurry up! Take a picture!"

Mom's yells brought me back to myself and I took out the camera and got it ready. Dad and I took turns taking pictures. Meanwhile the innkeeper came out and offered to take a picture of all of us. With the ocean behind her, Mom sat in her wheelchair with the two of us on either side of her. Dad and I crouched so that our heads would be on the same level, and Cabbage, who had finally woken up, made a face, then let out a big yawn from Mom's lap.

"OK, cheese!"

The owner of the inn snapped the shutter.

"Thank you!" we shouted in unison.

Then the innkeeper said, "One more!" and we lined up again, this time standing.

"OK, smile . . . Cheesecake!"

The innkeeper's earnest efforts to get us to smile, and his friendliness—which was just short of overbearing—made us all laugh, and just at that moment, the shutter snapped.

"Did you remember anything?"

I prodded Cabbage again after I finished my story.

"Apologies, old boy. I tried, but I just don't remember."

"That's too bad, Cabbage."

"I'm really sorry. I just can't help it. No matter how hard I try I can't remember anything. Except perhaps one thing . . ."

"One thing?"

"I was happy. That's all I remember."

"You were happy?"

"Yes. That's what I remember when I look at these photos. Simply that I was happy."

It seemed odd to me that Cabbage couldn't remember any of the details of the trip, not the inn, not even Mom herself, but that he could remember he'd been happy. But something in what Cabbage had said made me think, and then finally I realized . . . Mom didn't want that trip just for herself. She wanted me and Dad to make up.

I wondered why I'd never thought of that before. From the moment she gave birth to me, Mom gave me and Dad all of her time. I never imagined that when she had such little time left, she would still only be thinking of us. She didn't have to, but she devoted her life to us till the very end.

She had me completely fooled—it had taken me all this time to notice. I look back at the photos and notice the embarrassment on my father's face as he forces himself to smile. And me, with a face so much like my father's, also forcing an awkward smile. Then Mom sits between us grinning as if she couldn't be happier.

Looking at my mother's face, my heart grew heavy thinking of her and all she did for me. Suddenly I had tears rolling down my face, right there in front of Cabbage. My voice caught in my throat, and I stared silently at the photograph.

Cabbage had a look of concern on his face and came closer. He jumped into my lap and curled up there. My heart began to feel soothed as his warmth soaked into my body.

Cats are really something. They'll just ignore you half the time, but they seem to know when you're really in need of some comforting.

Just as cats don't have any sense of time, there must not be any such thing as loneliness for them either. There's just the time you spend alone and the time when you're with someone else. I suppose loneliness is another thing that only human beings feel. But looking at my mother's smiling face in those old photos makes me think that maybe it's only because we feel lonely that we have certain other feelings.

As I stroked his warm, furry body I decided to put some questions to Cabbage.

"Say, Cabbage, do you know what love is?"

"What's that, sir?"

"Well, I guess a cat wouldn't understand. It's something humans have. It's when you really like someone, and they're really important to you, and it makes you feel like you want to be with them all of the time."

"Is it a good thing?"

"Yeah. Though I guess it can also be a bit of a pain sometimes too, and then you feel like the other person is just a burden. But all in all it's a good thing."

Yes, that's it. We feel love. That's the expression Mom has on her face in that photograph. What else could you call it, apart from love? And this love, this thing unique to humans, even though it can sometimes be a burden or even get in your way, is something that buoys us human beings up. It's sort of like time in that way. It's one of those things that only exists for humans—like time, color, temperature, loneliness, and now love. All these things that only humans experience. In a way these things rule over or control us, but they also allow us to live fully. And they're precisely what makes us human.

No sooner had these thoughts occurred to me than my ears suddenly picked up something that sounded like a clock. But when I looked, just as before, no clock sat beside my bed.

Nevertheless, even though I couldn't see it with my eyes, I definitely got the feeling that there was something spurring me on. I started to get the sense that the endless ticking sound in my head might actually be the sound of the hearts of all the people in the world beating in time with one another.

Images occur to me in quick succession. In my mind's eye, I see the second hand of a stopwatch moving around the dial.

Then athletes sprinting the one hundred meters.

The second hand goes round and round the dial. Someone presses the button.

But the button is on an alarm clock.

The children who pressed the button crawl back under the bedcovers.

In their dreams they watch the hands of a large clock hanging on the wall go round and round the dial.

Then I see the clock tower lit up by the morning sun.

Young lovers wait for their dates below the clock tower.

I walk quickly past the lovers toward the tram stop, glancing at my watch.

As always, the tram is a bit late.

I arrive in front of a small clock-repair shop.

Countless clocks are laid out in the cramped space.

I hear them ticking. The sound fills the small space. The sound of time being carved up.

I stand still for a while, bending my ear toward the sound.

A sound I've heard constantly since the time I was small.

The sound that rules my life, but also gives me freedom.

Gradually the beating of my heart grows calm.

Then before long the sound fades into the distance, little by little, until it disappears.

"Well, Cabbage, I guess it's time to hit the sack."

I put the photo albums away and called Cabbage.

Cabbage let out a meow.

"Cabbage, what happened? Now you're acting like a cat again."

No sarcastic comments came back in the now-familiar outdated way of speaking.

Cabbage simply meowed. I had a bad feeling about this.

"Why, sir, are you disappointed?"

Suddenly from behind me there came a voice. Surprised, I turned around, and there stood Aloha. This time he wore a black Hawaiian shirt with an eerie-looking print—a picture of the ocean at night. He stood there with a big grin on his face.

"Might this be the end, sir?"

"That's not funny!"

"All right, all right, I'm sorry! I guess the magic spell didn't last as long as I expected. So he's back to being just a normal cat. Are you disappointed . . . sir?"

"Hey, give it a rest!"

"OK, I get it. But you know, the timing couldn't have been more perfect."

Aloha smiled again as he said this. It was that devilish smile. I knew I had seen it somewhere before. It was the look of someone with evil intentions—something else only humans are capable of.

"So, I've decided what I'm going to have you make disappear from the world next."

Aloha was still grinning that big silly grin.

I got the sense that something terrible was about to happen, and was beginning to find it difficult to breathe.

Imagination. Now, there's another thing that only human beings have.

Cruel images raced around in my head.

"Please stop!"

Without thinking about it, I cried out. Or no, it wasn't me but rather the Devil, who looked just like me.

"Makes you want to let out a cry just like that, right?"

Aloha laughed.

"Please . . . Just stop," I begged him, falling on my knees.

Then the Devil revealed his plan—

This time, let's make cats disappear from the world.

FRIDAY: IF CATS DISAPPEARED
FROM THE WORLD

His small body shook and he let out a painful meow. He wanted me to save him, but I could do nothing but watch him. Time and again Lettuce tried to stand on his own, but instantly collapsed.

"I guess this is it," I whispered.

"I guess so . . ."

There was a note of sad acceptance in Mom's quiet reply.

Five days had passed since Lettuce had lain down as if he were going to sleep. He couldn't eat anymore. Even presenting him with his favorite—fresh tuna—got no response out of him. Nor would he drink water. He slept for unusually long periods, and gradually we saw that he couldn't stand.

Even so, Lettuce tried over and over again to stand

up on his own. I had to give him water with an eye dropper because he couldn't drink on his own. With his strength slightly restored, he would immediately try to stand, but he was still a bit shaky on his feet and would soon lie down again. He always tried his hardest to stand on his own despite the fact that he didn't have the strength for it. Once he just about managed to pick up his feet and walk unsteadily right up to Mom, and then collapse in front of her.

"Lettuce!" I shouted, and rushed to pick him up. His body was warm, and he had become so thin he weighed practically nothing. His small body, with little strength left now, trembled ever so slightly. Lettuce hovered between life and death. You could tell he was scared—he couldn't understand what was happening to him. He didn't know that he was dying. After a while my arm started to ache, so I set him down on Mom's lap.

Now that he was comfortable, Lettuce began to purr. He let out as much of a meow as he was capable of producing, as if to announce that this was his spot. Mom was happy to have him there and stroked him gently. Gradually he closed his eyes and the trembling stopped. He seemed revived and raised his head for a moment, looking at us both with wide eyes. Finally, he took a deep breath and laid his head down on Mom's lap again where he became completely still, and didn't move again.

"Lettuce!"

I called his name, trying to convince myself he was only sleeping. Maybe I thought I could wake the dead if I simply repeated his name enough times, with just the right rhythm or emphasis.

"Be quiet," Mother said. "Don't say a word. He's gone to a place where there's no more pain."

Mom continued to stroke him gently as she said these words.

"It's all right now, it's all right . . . no more pain."

Mom rocked back and forth as she held the cat's still body, and the tears began to flow.

Finally the reality hit me. Lettuce was dead. He was really dead. I had to accept it. He was dead just like the rhinoceros beetles and crawdads I used to collect when I was little. After a while they'd just stop moving and that was that. In a daze I stroked his body. It was still soft and warm, and completely still.

I looked at the red collar Lettuce had worn for so long. He'd try to pull it off all the time, chewing away at it until it became worn out and ragged. Until a few moments ago it had seemed as if it too were something living, like Lettuce himself. But now suddenly it seemed like nothing more than a cold, lifeless object. Touching his collar gave me such a tangible feeling of death, I burst into tears as if to expel this unwelcome reality.

When I woke up I found that my eyes were filled with tears. It was still dark. Around 3am maybe. I looked beside me where Cabbage normally slept and saw that he was gone. I panicked and jumped out of bed, my eyes scanning the room. Then I saw Cabbage curled up asleep at the foot of the bed. As usual I hadn't slept well. But I was relieved to find that Cabbage was still there. The memory of the night before when Aloha suggested eliminating cats was still fresh in my mind.

So what would it be? My life or cats? At that moment, I couldn't imagine what my life would be like without Cabbage. Four years had passed since my mother had died. Cabbage had always been by her side. How could I erase him? What was I supposed to do?

If cats disappeared from the world, how would the world be different? What would be gained and what would be lost in a world without cats?

I remembered what my mother said a long time ago:

"Cats and humans have been partners for over ten thousand years. And what you realize when you've lived with a cat for a long time is that we may think we own them, but that's not the way it is. They simply allow us the pleasure of their company."

Cabbage was curled up and asleep. I lay down beside him and gazed at his face. Such a peaceful face. Never in his wildest dreams would he ever imagine a world where he had disappeared. I wouldn't be surprised if he woke up at this very moment, speaking like a gentleman and demanding to be fed. But as I stared at his sleeping face I could also imagine him saying like a faithful friend, "I would gladly disappear for you, sir."

On the one hand, they say that only humans have a concept of death. Cats don't see it coming. It doesn't cause them fear and anxiety like it does humans. And then humans end up keeping cats as pets, despite our angst over mortality, even though we know that the cat will die long before we do, causing the owner untold grief.

But then again, human beings can never grieve their own death. Death is always something that happens to others around them. When you boil it down, the death of a cat isn't so different from the death of a human.

When I thought about it this way I finally understood why it is that we humans keep cats as pets. There's a limit to how well we know ourselves. We don't know what we look like to others, and we can't know our own future, and we can't know what our own death will be like. And that's why we need cats. It's just like my mother said. Cats don't need us. It's human beings who need cats.

As these thoughts were going round and round in my brain I suddenly felt a sharp pain in the right side of my head.

Feeling powerless I curled up in bed, trembling, just like Lettuce when he was dying. I felt so small and helpless in this body of mine, this body now dominated by death. I felt a heavy weight pressing down on my chest.

The pain in my head was getting worse. I went into the kitchen and took two painkillers, washed them down with water, and then went back to bed. I fell into a deep sleep.

"So what are you going to do?"

I remembered Aloha's voice from the previous night.

"It's either your life or cats."

He laughed as he said the words.

"That shouldn't be such a hard choice, should it? After all, if you weren't around, who would take care of the cat? You don't have much to lose."

"Can you just give me some time?"

"What's there to think about? The answer's obvious."

"Just hold off for a second."

"OK. I get it. Then let me know your decision tomorrow . . . before your life is snuffed out."

With this, Aloha disappeared.

When I woke up the sun was shining brightly outside. It was morning. I took my time getting up, all the time looking around the room for Cabbage. He wasn't there. He was gone.

Where could he be? Had I decided to go ahead and make cats disappear while I was still half asleep?

I searched the room, first the old orange blanket he always slept in, then on top of the bookshelf, under the bed, the bathroom, the shower, but he was nowhere to be found. Cabbage liked crawling into confined spaces. Often he would hide in the washing machine, but he wasn't there either.

Finally I checked the window ledge. Cabbage always liked to perch there, his tail dangling and occasionally twitching. I thought of the curve of his back when he was curled up sleeping, and how the hum of his purring was carried on his breath. And how warm his body felt on my lap.

Finally I thought I heard a faint meow coming from somewhere outside.

"Cabbage . . . ?"

I ran out in a panic, shoving on a pair of sandals. I thought he might be underneath the white minivan that was always parked in the lot across the street, but he wasn't there either.

I ran along the route we took on our walk the day before. Maybe he was in the park . . . ? I ran up the hill until I made it to where we'd been yesterday. I thought he might be asleep on the park bench with the peeling blue paint. But no sign of Cabbage there. He wasn't at the noodle shop begging for bonito flakes either. So I turned and headed for the row of shops, but he wasn't there.

"Cabbage!"

I dashed around blindly, running and running until I'd worked up a terrible thirst. My throat and lungs felt so hot, like they might be about to combust. My leg muscles hurt so much I thought I might have torn them. I felt light-headed and a bit dizzy—reminding me of a day ages ago when I'd felt a similar combination of physical exhaustion and emotional pain. It's not something I wanted to ever think about again, but experiencing the same confusion of feelings must have triggered the memory.

★

It was four years ago. I remembered that day clearly, running as fast as I could to the hospital. My mother had had another seizure. She had already been in hospital for a long time, and would sleep for long stretches, but every now and again she would be woken up by a seizure. The hospital would always let me know, and I'd run back to be with her.

When I got there on that day, she was sitting up in her bed, in pain. She was shaking and saying over and over again that she was cold. Seeing her like that scared me, and I called out to her. I'd never seen her that way. The whole time I was growing up she was always so bright and cheerful, and warm. She was always on my side. I always felt completely safe and secure when she was near. And now she was going to leave me. I was so scared and upset I thought I was going to pass out. She was repeating something under her breath, it was almost impossible to understand. "Sorry . . . sorry, I'm so sorry to leave you alone." I was choked up—tears began to roll down my cheeks. I began to shake too, as I rubbed my mother's back.

She suffered like that for an hour and then they gave her an intravenous painkiller, which made her fall into a deep sleep. Now she was sleeping peacefully. So peacefully it was hard to believe she had just been in so much pain. I was relieved and sat down in the chair near the bedside, bone-tired. Soon I fell asleep too.

I had no idea how much time had passed, but when I woke up, Mom was sitting up in bed reading a book using a small portable lamp. Suddenly she was back to normal.

"Are you OK, Mom?"

"Oh, you're awake. Yes, I'm OK now."

"Good."

". . . I wonder what's going to happen to me."

Mom examined her wrist. She had become so thin.

"I've become just like Lettuce."

"Mom, you shouldn't say that!"

"You're right. I'm sorry."

The window of the hospital room faced west, and the setting sun glowed bright pink, even brighter and more beautiful than it usually did. There was a photograph on Mom's bedside. It was one of the photos we'd taken on our trip to the hot spring. Mom and Dad and me all facing the camera, smiling with our backs to the ocean.

"The trip to the hot spring was wonderful."

"Yeah, it really was."

"I was wondering what was going to happen when we didn't get the inn we wanted."

"Yeah, I really panicked."

"Looking back now it seems kind of funny."

"Yeah, it does."

"The sashimi was delicious."

"We should go again."

"Yes, we should. But I don't think that's really a possibility."

Mom spoke matter-of-factly, mentioning several times that she thought it wouldn't happen. I couldn't find it in me to respond to what she was saying.

"So I guess Dad hasn't come, right?"

I couldn't take the silence over that elephant in the room anymore.

"No, I guess not . . ."

"I told him he should come, but he just said that he'd visit after he finished repairing the watch he was working on."

"Oh, did he . . ."

Mom had a favorite wristwatch that she wore all the time. It was that watch that Dad was repairing. It was the only wristwatch she ever owned . . . which was kind of odd when you consider the fact that she'd married a man who repaired clocks for a living.

"What's so special about that watch?"

"It's the first present your father ever gave me."

"Oh, so that's it."

"He made it himself using antique parts from his collection."

"So he actually did something nice for once?"

"He did. You know, he's really very sweet. He just finds it difficult to express himself."

Mom sounded so young when she talked about Dad like this, erupting in girlish laughter.

"Last week your father came to see me, and I told him my watch wasn't running. So he just took it with him when he left, without saying anything. I guess he planned on repairing it."

"But why decide to do it now of all times?"

"Don't worry about it. I'm happy *you're* here, but people are different. There are different ways of showing you love someone."

"I don't know . . ."

"That's just the way it is."

It was the last time we ever spoke. Soon after that, she took a turn for the worse and within an hour she was dead.

I called the shop over and over again, but Dad didn't come. He finally arrived half an hour after she'd died. He held Mom's wristwatch in his hands. He hadn't been able to get it going again. Mom's lifeless body lay there, still, and I cursed him. Why now? Why at a time like this? I just couldn't understand him, however Mom tried to explain it.

They took Mom to the funeral home, leaving the hospital room empty and still. Where Mom had been there was only a clean white sheet . . . It was more than I could take. On the bedside sat her wristwatch. She always had it on her. It was like a part of her body. And now all the life had gone out of it. The wristwatch had become a piece of useless rubbish. Suddenly I remembered Lettuce's red collar, and the thought of it made the pain even worse. I picked the watch up and held it close to my heart, and found myself sobbing there, alone.

I never spoke to my father again, after that day.

Even now I can't say how things got so bad between me and my father. We used to be a happy family. We were close. We would go out to eat together and go on holiday. But somehow over time, for no reason I could think of, the foundations that my relationship with my father was built on simply rotted away.

But we're family. You just take it for granted that they'll always be there and that you'll muddle along somehow. I always believed that. I never questioned such an obvious assumption. But ironically enough, because we both believed in this unspoken truth, my father and I never bothered to talk to each other, to ask how the other was feeling, or what they were thinking about. We both went on believing that whatever we felt as individuals must be the way it really was.

But it doesn't work that way. Instead of thinking of family as just being there, you need to think of it as something you do. Family is a verb—you "do family." My father and I were two separate individuals who just happened to be related by blood. And because we accepted and lived with the distance that had grown between us for so long, eventually the last thread connecting us broke.

Even when Mom got sick my father and I never spoke to each other. We both put our own needs and what we were going through first. We didn't think about Mom and what she needed. Even as Mom started to feel worse and worse, she carried on doing the housework, and though I think part of me knew, I still didn't take her to see the doctor. I just blamed my father for expecting her to continue doing the housework, even in her condition. And I suppose he blamed *me* for not taking her to see the doctor. When the end came, I only cared about being by Mom's side, while the only thing Dad seemed to care about was repairing her watch. Even Mom's death couldn't bring us together.

I ran and ran with no idea where I was going, and I still couldn't find Cabbage anywhere. Had cats really disappeared from the world? Had I made Cabbage disappear? Would I never see Cabbage again? Would I never get to touch his soft fur again, to feel his warmth against my body, touch his dangling tail or his fleshy paws, or feel the thumping of his little heart?

Now both Mom and Lettuce were gone, and maybe Cabbage was gone too. I didn't want to be left alone. I was grief-stricken, angry, anxious, and in pain. My eyes began to fill with tears. I kept on running, forcing my legs to keep moving, panting now, my mouth open and dry. I ran and ran until my head started to hurt again and I collapsed onto the cold stone pavement. I carried on, crawling awkwardly on the ground.

Then I recognized the paving stones. I looked up and realized that I had reached the square where I met my old girlfriend the other day. I'd just run the same distance it took the tram thirty minutes to complete. I was too late. The feel of the cold stone pavement brought reality crashing down on me. I had eliminated cats. I had made Cabbage disappear from the world.

But just then I heard a meow. I thought I could make it out, coming from a distance. I stood up mechanically. Then I heard it again. I ran toward the sound. Was I dreaming? Or was it real? My head was spinning and I couldn't think straight. I forced myself to run even though my feet felt like lead weights. Following the meowing I found myself standing in front of a red-brick building. It was the movie theater.

Again the same meow. Cabbage was there, on the counter in the movie theater. In the same position he always adopted, he was stretched out with his tail dangling over the counter's edge. He jumped gracefully onto the floor and walked toward me, letting out another meow. I picked him up and squeezed him tight. Feeling his soft fur and hearing him purr gave me the sense that this was what life was all about.

"It's good you two found each other again."

There she stood in front of us. Of course. My ex-girlfriend. She lived here, after all.

"I was so surprised when Cabbage turned up here on his own."

"Thank you. I'm so relieved."

"And there you go crying again. You haven't changed at all, have you?"

Only then did I realize that tears were streaming down my face. It was embarrassing, but I was just too happy for words. Cabbage hadn't disappeared. He was back in my arms. I wiped the tears away and got back to my feet.

"Well, this must have been your mother's doing."

"What do you mean?"

She handed me a letter. It was addressed to me. It had a stamp, but no postmark, meaning that it had never been sent. Someone wrote it but then never mailed it.

"It's from your mother. She had me keep it for you."

"From Mom?"

"That's right. Back when your mother was in the hospital I paid her a visit, and she asked me to hold on to it."

I had no idea until now that my old girlfriend had visited my mother when she was in the hospital. I was finding it hard to believe, but took the letter from her anyway.

"Your mother wrote you the letter while she was in hospital, but she just couldn't send it. She was afraid that she would never see you again once you'd read it. So she

171

asked me to give it to you if you were ever going through a really hard time."

"I see . . ."

"At first I turned her down because I had broken up with you years before, and I didn't expect to see you again. But then she said it didn't matter if you never got it. She just wanted someone to have the letter. And then, when I saw that Cabbage had turned up here today and that you were beside yourself in tears, I realized that it was time to give you the letter."

"Now?"

"She did say to give it to you if you were going through a difficult time."

"Right . . ."

"Your mother was really great. She just knew things. It was like she had magical powers or something."

Hearing herself say this, she laughed.

I sat down on the sofa in the theater lobby and put Cabbage on my lap.

Then I carefully opened the letter. On the top of the first page in large letters (she had beautiful handwriting) it said: "Ten things I want to do before I die." The title was a bit of an anticlimax. So both mother and son, without knowing it, had written the same thing. I couldn't help but laugh and carried on to the second page.

I don't have much longer to live, so I thought I'd note down ten things I'd like to do before I die. I'd like to travel, and enjoy delicious gourmet meals, and I'd like to kit myself out in some really stylish clothes. But then, as I wrote these things I began to wonder. Was this really the kind of thing that was important to me? Is this really what I want to do before I die? I started a new list when suddenly I realized that all of the things I wanted to do before I died were for you. Your life will go on for many years beyond mine, and in the course of that life there'll be both good times and bad. You'll experience joy, but there will also be times of sadness and pain. So I decided to write down ten beautiful things about you so that whenever you're going through a difficult time, you'll be given the courage and self-belief to go on.

So instead of a list of ten things I want to do before I die, this is what I wrote.

Things that are beautiful and good about you:

When people are sad, you're able to cry along with them.

173

And when people are happy you're able to share their joy with them.

You look really sweet when you're asleep.

Your dimples when you smile.

Your habit of rubbing your nose when you're worried or anxious.

Your concern for the needs of others.

Whenever I caught a cold you helped with the housework, and acted like you enjoyed doing it.

You always ate whatever I cooked as if it were the most delicious thing in the world.

How you'd think deeply and ponder over things.

And after all that brooding you always seemed to come up with the best solution to the problem.

As you go on with your life, always remember the things that are good in you. They're your gifts. As long as you have these things, you'll find happiness, and you'll make the people around you happy. Thank you for everything you've done for me. And goodbye. I hope you always keep hold of these things that are so beautiful about you.

The tears rolled down and fell on the letter like warm, salty drops of rain. I quickly wiped them off, not wanting to ruin a letter that mattered so much. But when I tried to stop I just cried more and more, and the letter got wetter and wetter, the ink beginning to smudge. Along with the tears, came a torrent of memories of my mother.

Whenever I caught cold my mother would rub my back. Once I got lost when we were at an amusement park and began to cry. I remember how my mother ran to me, and picked me up and held me. When I wanted the same kind of lunch box as all the other kids, my mother ran around town all day long to find just the right one. I always fidgeted when I was asleep, and my mother would come in and put the covers back on. She always bought me new clothes when I needed them and never bought anything for herself. She made the best Japanese rolled omelet. I could never eat enough of it and she'd give me her portion. For her birthday I gave her a voucher for a shoulder massage, but she never used it. She said it was too much of a treat for her and didn't want to waste it. She bought a piano and played my favorite songs for me, but she wasn't very good and always tripped up and made mistakes in the same places.

My mother . . . Did she have any hobbies of her own? Did she have any time to herself? Were there things she wanted to do, hopes and dreams? I wanted to at least thank her, but never found the words. I never even bought her flowers because it seemed cheesy. Why couldn't I at least have done something small? It was such a simple thing. And when she finally left this world it came as such a shock. I hadn't ever imagined that she would die.

"In order to gain something you have to lose something."

My mother's words came back to me.

Mom, I don't want to die. I'm afraid of dying. But it's just like you used to say.

Stealing things from others in order to live is even more painful.

"Come now, sir, dry those eyes."

I heard a voice and looked around. Cabbage was curled up on my lap looking at me. Suddenly he could speak again, and I was surprised. He still had that haughty tone of voice.

"It's terribly simple. All you need to do is make cats disappear."

"No, Cabbage, I can't do that!"

"Why, if it were up to me, I'd have you live, sir. It shan't be easy for me when you're no longer with us."

I never thought the day would come when I'd be moved to tears by the words of a cat. But I had a feeling he would have been able to communicate just as well with a meow and a purr. Just when I thought I'd calmed down, I began to tear up again.

"Oh, do please stop crying. My existence is a trifle compared to what you have already made disappear."

"No, Cabbage, no. It doesn't have to be that way."

If cats disappeared from the world . . .

If Lettuce *and* Cabbage and Mom disappeared . . . I just couldn't imagine it. I may not be the smartest guy, but I felt like I was beginning to understand. There's a reason that things exist in this world. And there's no reason good enough for making them disappear.

I'd made my decision. And I think that Cabbage above all understood my resolve. He was silent for a while, and then began to speak again.

"I understand, sir."

"Thank you."

"Now, just one more thing."

"One more thing?"

"Close your eyes."

"What for?"

"Never mind. Just close them."

So I closed my eyes, and out of the darkness a figure appeared—it was my mother. Oh sweet memory . . . a memory of childhood.

When I was little I would get upset all the time, and wouldn't calm down or stop crying. Then my mother would say softly, and gently, "Close your eyes."

"Why?"

"Never mind. Just close them."

So I closed my eyes, still crying. In the darkness my emotions became a black whirlpool swirling round and round.

"What do you feel?"

"Sad and upset, Mama."

I slowly opened my eyes, and my mother went on as she gazed at me.

"All right, next make a happy face."

"I can't."

"Go ahead. Even if you have to force it."

My mind and body were at odds with each other. I couldn't smile very well. I managed to twist my unwilling face into a smile, but I still felt bad. The tears didn't stop.

The sound of my mother's voice saying "take your time" soothed me, and I managed to force a smile.

"OK now, close your eyes again."

Prompted by my mother, I slowly shut my eyes. When I tried closing my eyes while smiling, no matter how forced it was, I could feel my emotions being soothed. The black whirlpool disappeared and what looked like a rising sun began to appear in the darkness. Gradually this gentle, cream-colored light would spread all around. I could feel my heart finally begin to warm as the light grew stronger and I was wrapped up in a feeling of tenderness.

"How do you feel now?"

"I'm OK now."

"Good. I'm glad."

"Mama, how did you do that?"

"It's a secret."

"What do you mean?"

"It's a little magic trick you can play on yourself. Whenever you feel sad and lonely, just smile and close your eyes. Do it as many times as you have to."

So it was Cabbage who'd reminded me of my mother's magic. Whenever I felt bad I would beg her to do it. There in the lobby of the movie theater, as I sat on the sofa, I slowly closed my eyes and forced myself to smile. The warmth crept back into my heart, and I felt calmed and soothed. It seemed I still had some of Mom's magic left in me after all.

"Thank you, Mother."

I'd never been able to say that to her. Those simple words. But I really did want to say it. And I finally had.

I opened my eyes, and Cabbage was still there, curled up purring on my lap.

"Thank you, Cabbage."

I stroked his fur some more and he meowed as if he'd understood what I'd said. Then he meowed some more. He seemed to be trying very hard to tell me something. The strange human speech, those expressions that came out of some old TV show were no more. It seemed to me like this was his way of saying goodbye.

I remembered again what Mom used to always say about cats:

"We may think we own cats but that's not the way it is. They simply allow us the pleasure of their company."

I'm glad I had a chance to talk to Cabbage before it all ended. Maybe this was Mom's magic too. Goodbye, Cabbage. Thank you for the time you gave me.

I stayed there for a while longer, sitting on the sofa of the theater lobby in the fading light. I read back over the letter again as I stroked Cabbage. I read it again and again. But each time there was something at the end of the letter I got stuck on, like being pricked by a thorn. I felt a little stab of pain in my heart. There was still one thing I had left to do.

This is what it said at the end of the letter:

"Please make up with your father. I want you two to get along."

SATURDAY: IF I DISAPPEARED

FROM THE WORLD

I don't know whether I'm happy or unhappy. But there's one thing I do know. You can convince yourself to be happy or unhappy. It just depends on how you choose to see things.

When I woke up the next morning Cabbage was asleep next to me. I could feel his soft fur, and hear his little heart beating away. So cats hadn't disappeared from the world. That meant that *I* was going to disappear from the world.

If I disappeared from the world . . . I tried to imagine what it would be like. I suppose it wouldn't be the worst thing to have ever happened. Everyone dies eventually. The fatality rate is 100%. So when you think about it in that way, whether it's a happy death or an unhappy death depends on how you've lived your life.

Again my mother's words came back to me:

"In order to gain something you have to lose something."

In exchange for my life, I made mobile phones, movies, and clocks disappear from the world, but I couldn't bring myself to get rid of cats. I realize that it might seem stupid for me to give up my own life for cats. But that's just the way it is. It's who I am. There was a real possibility that I was some kind of idiot, but I really don't get any satisfaction out of extending my life in exchange for other people losing something they hold very dear. For me, cats are no different from the sun and the ocean and the air we breathe. So I have decided to stop making things disappear from the world. I have decided to accept the life that has been given to me exactly as it is, even though it seemed like it would be on the rather short side. So that means that I'm going to die soon.

When Cabbage and I got home last night Aloha was waiting for us. He wore his usual loud outfit—Hawaiian shirt and shorts, with a pair of sporty sunglasses perched on his forehead. I was annoyed to see him, but on the other hand, a part of me found seeing the same old outfit almost reassuring. It's kind of frightening how easily you get used to things.

"Hey, where the hell were you? I thought maybe you'd been spirited away or something. I was about to lodge a missing person's report with the man upstairs."

"Sorry."

"Whoa there, what happened? Lost your mojo? You gotta jump right in there and get back into the groove."

"I'm sorry."

"It's OK, it's OK. No worries. Let's just get on with it. Time to erase . . . you know what . . ."

Aloha pointed his finger at Cabbage and began humming a cheerful tune.

"I won't do it."

"Huh?"

"I said I won't do it. I won't make cats disappear."

"Are you serious?"

"Yes. I'm serious."

I looked at Aloha's surprised expression and couldn't help laughing.

"What's so funny? You're gonna die, man. Are you sure about this?"

"Yes. I'm OK with that. I'm not going to make any more things disappear."

"But you can live a lot longer."

Aloha looked disappointed.

"Yeah, but just being alive doesn't mean all that much on its own. How you live is more important."

Aloha retreated into silence. Then after staring at my face for a long time he opened his mouth to speak.

"Well . . . looks like I've lost to God again. Man, humans! Can't do anything with them."

"What's wrong?"

"Oh, nothing . . . forget it. It's my loss. Go ahead and die if you want to!"

"Hey, that's not nice! Although of course, I *am* going to die."

I laughed, and then Aloha started to laugh too.

"Well, I guess we'll be going our separate ways now, huh?"

"Yes, that's right."

"Strangely enough, I'm kind of sad."

"Yeah, me too. You were a really interesting guy."

"You too . . . a real funny devil!"

"Don't get me started!"

"By the way, what does the Devil normally look like?"

"You really want to know?"

"Yes, I do."

"Well, actually, I don't really have any one specific form."

"What do you mean?"

"The Devil only exists in the hearts and minds of humans. Then you humans express that in lots of different forms. It's kind of random. Like with horns and a pitchfork, or in the form of a dragon."

"Ah, I see now."

"Though I take particular exception to the horns and pitchfork—I mean, give me a break! It's just bad taste, don't you think?"

"Yeah, you're right about that one."

"I don't like that look at all."

"I'm not surprised."

"So you see, the form I take all depends on your imagination. The devil in *your* heart looks just like you."

"But your personality is totally different to mine."

"Hmmm, yes. But I think that's the important bit. In other words, I'm the person you could have been."

"In what sense?"

"It's the side of yourself that you never showed. You know, cheerful but shallow, wearing flashy clothes, doing whatever you wanted without worrying about what other people would think—saying whatever you want, no matter how inappropriate."

"Yeah . . . the total opposite of me."

"Right. I'm made up of all those little regrets in life. Like, what if, whenever you reached a fork in the road in life, you'd gone the other way? What would have happened? Who would you have become? That's what the Devil is all about. It's what you wanted to become but couldn't. It's both the closest thing and the farthest thing from who you are."

"So . . . do you think I turned out OK?"

"Hey, I'm not exactly the best person to be putting that question to!"

"I wonder if I'll have any regrets when it comes time to die."

"Oh, of course you will. You want to live, right? You might even beg the Devil to come back! Humans tend to regret the life they never lived, the choices they never made."

Those who know they will die tomorrow live to the fullest in the limited time they have.

That's what some people say, but I tend to disagree. When a person becomes aware of their impending death, they have to make a compromise between the life they wish they could have led, and the reality of death. Sure there are all the little regrets, the broken dreams, but you have to go easy on yourself, and be flexible. Having had the chance to make things disappear from the world in order to gain just one more day of life, I've come to realize that there's a certain beauty in those regrets. Because it's proof of having lived. I won't eliminate anything more from the world. And I may regret it at the moment I actually die, but that's OK with me. No matter how you look at it, life is full of regrets anyway.

I was never able to be completely myself or live my life in exactly the way I wanted to. I'm not sure I ever even figured out what exactly "being myself" really meant. So I'll die with all those failures and regrets, all those unfulfilled dreams—all the people I never met, the things I never tasted, the places I've never been. But that doesn't bother me anymore. I'm satisfied with who I am and how I've lived. I'm happy to have been here at all. Where else but here could I have been?

The last week has been so strange—first finding out I didn't have long to live, and then the Devil appearing, and making things disappear from the world in order to give me another day of life. It's kind of like the apple that was offered to Adam and Eve, a bet between God and the Devil. Maybe what God was really asking me to consider wasn't the value of the things I was making disappear, but the value of my own life.

God created the world in six days, and in the same number of days I went and made things disappear, one at a time. But I couldn't bring myself to make cats disappear, and instead I decided that *I* would become no more. And soon I'll have my day of rest too.

Seeing me deep in thought like this the Devil laughed at me.

"In the end you came to know exactly how wonderful life is. You became aware of who the most important people to you are, and the value of lots of other important, irreplaceable things. You traveled around the world you live in and saw it anew. And you found that despite the boredom and routine of that world, there is a real beauty in it. That on its own makes my having come here worth it."

"But I'm going to die soon."

"Probably so. But one thing's for sure. You're happy now that you've realized that."

"I wish I would have realized that sooner."

"Yeah, but no one really knows exactly how long their life will be. It could be another few days or it could be a

189

few months. It's the same with everyone. No one knows exactly how long they're going to live."

"Yes, I suppose so."

"So there's really no such thing as too late or too soon."

"That's a nice way of thinking about it."

"Don't you think so? Anyway, I just thought I'd throw that in as an extra freebie since this is the last time we'll be seeing each other. Make sure the last thing you do is done with passion. Go all the way! Well, it's time now. Goodbye!"

Aloha said goodbye in his usual complete lack of seriousness, he gave me a wink (that is, his poor imitation of a wink) and then he was gone. Cabbage let out a sad-sounding meow.

Then I began to get my affairs in order. I was preparing to die. First I cleaned my room and threw away anything unnecessary. I got rid of embarrassing diaries, out-of-date clothing, and photos I hadn't been able to part with until now. Fragments of my life appearing and then dis-appearing. I wondered whether Aloha would have given me an extension on my life if I had thrown away things like this. But anyway, I had no regrets. I was relieved now that I didn't need to make anything else disappear. I threw away all kinds of things that brought back memories while Cabbage did his best to get in the way. By the time I was done it was evening.

Orange rays of light spilled in through the window, landing on the metallic box sitting on top of the dining-room table. I'd found the box deep inside the wardrobe. It was a shabby old thing that had, at one time, contained cookies. It was my box of treasures from when I was a little kid. I stared at it for a while. It held things that were important to me at one time, and I'd completely forgotten about its existence. Whatever was in it, I probably wouldn't consider it treasure at this point in my life.

People are fickle that way. Something they once valued becomes meaningless to them almost overnight. Even the most treasured presents, letters, and beautiful memories are forgotten about, becoming useless odds and ends. Long ago I had sealed my treasures in this box along with my memories. I hesitated over opening it. I couldn't do it. I went out instead.

I left the apartment and headed to the funeral home. I decided to plan my own service. The funeral home was on the far edge of town and had an elegant ceremonial hall, showing just how lucrative this business was. I talked to the salesman and discussed their various packages. The salesman was warm and understanding when I explained my circumstances, and went through the fees for the various items. I would have to buy a portable Buddhist altar, a coffin, flowers, a portrait of myself to display by the coffin, an urn for my ashes, a Buddhist tablet, a hearse, and of course I'd have to pay for the cremation. It all came to 1,500,000 yen. This is how much it would cost for one small funeral, which I was obviously paying for myself. Everything cost something —the cotton stuffed in the corpse's nose, the dry ice placed in the coffin, and so on. The blow-by-blow explanation seemed to go on and on.

The dry ice alone (put in the coffin so that the body won't decay) would cost 8,400 yen per day. So stupid! Each of the items was ranked with a breakdown of the price given. Even after death there's a scale you're graded against! What awful creatures we humans are!

But it doesn't stop there. You can also go for options like natural wood, or it can be carved, lined with suede, or even lacquered—cost per item anything from 50,000 to 1,000,000 yen!

The salesman led me into a dimly lit room where they displayed the coffins. I tried to imagine myself inside of one of those things. My funeral. But who would come? Let's see . . . friends, former lovers, relatives, former teachers, colleagues . . . and how many of these people would *really* grieve for me? And when it came time for the eulogy, what would they say about me?

He was a nice and funny guy, or he was lazy, impatient, hot-headed, unpopular, a loser who couldn't get a date.

What will they talk about? What memories will they share as they gather around my casket?

Thinking about this I started to wonder. What had I given to the people around me while I was alive? What would I be leaving behind? My whole life will be summed up in those moments that I won't be around to see—the time after I'm dead. In all the thirty years I'd been alive this was the first time I'd ever thought about this. My whole existence had taken place within this little sliver of time that sat between two much larger chunks of time— during which I didn't exist. It's been within this narrow slice that I have made my mark . . . for whatever it's worth.

I returned home to a space that, after the cleaning and organizing, seemed as if it had been hollowed out. Cabbage came up to me and meowed again and again, as if complaining about having been left alone there. The apartment was so empty now, there was something eerie about it. I placed the raw tuna I'd bought at the fish shop in the old shopping district on a plate. Cabbage signaled his pleasure with an odd-sounding meow as if to say, "Indeed, you have finally gathered my meaning!" Then he started gobbling down the tuna.

While Cabbage was busy eating I picked up the old cookie container on the table and stared at it for a while. Then finally I opened it. This is where I kept all my hopes and dreams as a boy. It was my stamp collection.

There were stamps of all colors and sizes from around the world. All at once the memories began flooding in. They were memories of my father. When I was a small boy my father bought me a collection of Olympic commemorative stamps. They were small and colorful, and too special to use for mailing letters. After that, my father often brought me presents of stamps. Small and large stamps, Japanese stamps and stamps from foreign countries. My father was so shy and reserved, he rarely spoke. So the stamps became a kind of way for us to communicate. It's strange, but it's almost as if I understood what he was thinking about depending on the kind of stamps he gave me.

When I was in elementary school my father traveled to Europe with a group of friends. He sent postcards from all of the places he visited. There were large, colorful stamps on the postcards. The one I remember most clearly had a picture of a cat yawning. It made me laugh. It looked just like Lettuce. It was one of the few jokes my father ever came up with. It made me happy, and I removed the stamp by soaking the postcard in water overnight. I added it to my collection. I couldn't sleep that night imagining all the places my father had visited in Europe. I imagined him on a street corner in Paris, buying the cat stamp at a shop, speaking in stilted French, and then sitting in a cafe writing the postcard. I even imagined him dropping the card into a yellow mailbox, and then the postman collecting it, taking it to the airport where it was loaded with other mail heading for Japan. And then finally the postcard would be delivered to my own town and then to our house. The entire journey of the postcard after it had been posted fascinated me.

Finally I understood why I ended up being a postman. I would spend ages gazing at the stamps, all the different colors and the many countries they'd come from. There were all kinds of pictures and designs on the stamps.

Pictures of people and places I could only imagine. They became really precious to me.

Then I thought about all the things I might have made disappear from the world if I'd gone on with the Devil's deal. Maybe the world wouldn't have changed that much without these things in it, but at the same time, it's all these individual objects, along with all the other things that exist, that make up this world. That's what occurred to me as I held these little squares cut out of paper. Somehow I began to feel like the whole process of placing a stamp on an envelope and mailing it, it arriving at its destination, had a deeper meaning. Just imagining it gave me a certain warm, happy feeling.

Then I realized what I needed to do in the time left to me. I needed to write you a letter. I needed to write about all the things I'd never told you these past years. The thousands of words that lay dormant within me, all the greetings I never sent your way, the emotions I never shared. I let all my feelings flow out of me onto the paper, and put a stamp on it. I imagine all the stamps scattering and falling like flower petals, decorating my final moments.

So many stamps with so many pictures: a festival, a horse, a gymnast, and a dove; a Japanese woodblock print, and an ocean. A piano, a car, people dancing, and flowers, great men remembered by their various nations. An airplane, a ladybug, a desert, and a yawning cat. At the moment of my death when I lie down and close my eyes. All of them swirl round and round above me. A phone rings, and on the screen an old silent movie plays—*Limelight*, then the hands of the clock begin to move, and all the letters fly through the air. Red, blue, yellow, and green, purple, white, and pink. The many-colored envelopes flutter away into the pale-blue sky. And quietly, I breathe my last. Before the myriad of stamps, and the letters expressing endless pain, but also unlimited happiness, in all my smallness, alone, I die with a faint smile on my face.

So now I sit down to write a letter. A letter which is also my last will and testament. Who should I address my last letter to? I ponder this for a while when Cabbage comes up to me and meows. Ah yes, that's it. Now I know. I will address my letter to the same person that I'll deliver Cabbage to before I die. There's only one person it can be. Maybe I've known for a long time, but couldn't admit it to myself.

On the day Mom found Cabbage, when she brought him in out of the rain, I was against the whole thing at first.

Someday the cat was going to die and once again Mom would be devastated. I didn't want her to feel so sad again so at first I didn't think we should take in another cat. But you, Dad, felt differently.

"Why not keep it," you said. "We all die eventually anyway, both humans and cats. Once you understand and accept that, it's OK."

Somewhere deep inside I always knew that in your own way, you did care about Mom's needs. And you even felt something for Lettuce, our first cat, even though you didn't show it the same way everyone else did. I realize now that I was wrong about you. You always said the right thing, and you were honest. I wonder if there was something about that that made me reject you.

I didn't know how to respond, and fell silent. Then the kitten mewed and walked on its still-unsteady feet to you, Father, and you picked it up and stroked it. I remembered you would do the same with Lettuce. Mom smiled when she saw this, and when you saw that Mom was happy, you brightened up too.

"He looks just like Lettuce, doesn't he?"

"Yes, he does."

"Then we'll call him Cabbage."

After you said this you looked all embarrassed and

handed the kitten to me. Then you went back to your shop, sat down at your desk, and carried on repairing clocks.

You were the one who named Cabbage. So I'm leaving Cabbage with you, Dad.

So then I began writing this letter. My first and last letter to you, Father. It's gotten pretty long . . . A long, long will and testament. It's because there's so much I needed to tell you, starting with the strange events of the past week, and then things about Mom, and Cabbage. There are things I've wanted to tell you for so long now, about me for instance.

I place a clean white sheet of paper on the desk and begin to write. At the top of the page I write –

Dear Father . . .

SUNDAY: GOODBYE WORLD

Morning came. The letter lay on the desk in front of me, finally finished. I'd written and written without eating or drinking, with Cabbage occasionally interfering by jumping up on the desk and walking on the letter as I tried to write. And now that I'm done, I've put the letter in an overly large envelope, and carefully picked out the stamps from my old collection. I chose a stamp with a picture of a sleeping cat on it, and stuck it to the envelope.

I picked up Cabbage and left the apartment. It was early morning and still a bit chilly as I made my way down the hill to the nearest mailbox. The red mailbox with its large mouth was waiting for me. It's the perfect ending. Or at least it should have been. I post the letter, my father gets it, opens the envelope, and reads the letter. And in this way my father gets to know what I was thinking and feeling.

*

But something just wasn't right. I stood staring blankly at the gaping mouth of the mailbox and then had second thoughts. I immediately turned and retraced my steps, back up the hill with Cabbage in tow, and back to the apartment. Out of breath from the exertion, I opened the closet and pulled out some clothes. A white shirt, striped tie, and charcoal-grey suit. It was my postman's uniform. I put it on and looked at myself briefly in the mirror. The figure in the mirror looked a lot like my father. Over time, I had come to look just like my father. My face, posture, and gestures had all come to look just like the father I'd hated so much for so long.

My father who sat for hours hunched over his desk repairing clocks, the same father who squeezed my hand tight in the movie theater, who bought me stamps, who held Cabbage, smiling, when he was a kitten, and who ran through the hot-spring town with me, looking for a vacancy. The same father who arrived late at Mom's funeral and sat alone in a corner crying and trying to hide his tears.

On the day I left home my father left my treasure box in the middle of my empty room. Now I remember that my father had stretched out his hand to me as I was about to leave. All I had to do was take that hand. I should have taken it, as he had mine in the movie theater when I was still small.

Father—

All these years I really wanted to see you. I wanted to say I'm sorry. I wanted to say thank you, and goodbye. I felt the tears beginning to run down my cheeks. I wiped them on the sleeve of my postman's uniform and put the letter in my bag, then I ran out of the apartment. I clattered down the stairs and got on the bicycle I'd left at the bottom. I put Cabbage in the basket and sped down the hill. It was hard pedaling and the frame of the old bicycle squeaked. The tears ran down my face as I pedaled, and soon I reached the next hill, which I had to climb.

The wind began to blow. The sky cleared and I got the feeling that spring was on its way, the warm rays of the sun enveloping me. Cabbage was enjoying the wind in his face and let out a meow. Directly below me I could see the dark blue of the ocean. My father lived on the other side of the bay. I often looked down on that town from the top of the hill. It was so close, yet I'd never gone to visit him. That's where I was headed. To the neighboring town to see my father. I pedaled hard, and then coasted downhill, gradually speeding up. Faster and faster I went as I got closer to my father's house.